YOU NEED A LADDER

Eleanor turned as Geoffrey spoke, a rush of color on her cheeks. Foolish to think it could be a flush of pleasure at seeing him.

"I . . . I came out to fetch some . . . some greenery. For Emma," she said in a rush.

He raised his eyebrows at that hasty explanation. So, it was not the cold that had stained her cheeks. She seemed embarrassed. But over what?

He glanced up at the clump of soft green that dangled above her reach, its white, waxy berries now visible to him. A smile edged his mouth as he realized why she blushed.

"Greenery? A general sort of greenery, or did you have something specific in mind?" he asked, unable to resist teasing. She deserved some sort of punishment for worrying him by going out on her own.

"Mistletoe, actually. Emma swears we cannot have a proper Christmas without it. She sent me out to find some."

She said it as if daring him to even suggest that it had been her idea to search for a kissing bough. And he knew then that she deserved far more punishment than a mere teasing

He pulled off one glove and reached up, stretching only a little to easily pluck down the clump of mistletoe that twined around the oak in its ancient mating of vine to tree. Then he offered it to her—only when he put it into her hand, he did not let go of it, but stared down at her, an odd light in his eyes.

"The old way is that a man should pluck a berry when he kisses a girl under a kissing bough. And when the berry is gone, there should be no more kissing."

Fascinated by the sparkling light in his eyes which shone like sunlight off a lake, she stared up at him, her lips parted and dry, and her heart thudding.

"We ought to keep the old customs alive, don't you think?" he said, and then he swept off his hat and lowered his mouth to hers.

BOOK YOUR PLACE ON OUR WEBSITE AND MAKE THE READING CONNECTION!

We've created a customized website just for our very special readers, where you can get the inside scoop on everything that's going on with Zebra, Pinnacle and Kensington books.

When you come online, you'll have the exciting opportunity to:

- View covers of upcoming books

- Read sample chapters

- Learn about our future publishing schedule (listed by publication month *and author*)

- Find out when your favorite authors will be visiting a city near you

- Search for and order backlist books from our online catalog

- Check out author bios and background information

- Send e-mail to your favorite authors

- Meet the Kensington staff online

- Join us in weekly chats with authors, readers and other guests

- Get writing guidelines

- AND MUCH MORE!

**Visit our website at
http://www.zebrabooks.com**

Under the Kissing Bough

Shannon Donnelly

ZEBRA BOOKS
Kensington Publishing Corp.
http://www.zebrabooks.com

ZEBRA BOOKS are published by

Kensington Publishing Corp.
850 Third Avenue
New York, NY 10022

All Kensington titles, imprints, and distributed lines are
available at special quantity discounts for bulk purchases for
sales promotion, premiums, fund-raising, educational or in-
stitutional use.

Special book excerpts or customized printings can also be
created to fit specific needs. For details, write or phone the
office of the Kensington Special Sales Manager: Kensington
Publishing Corp., 850 Third Avenue, New York, NY 10022.
Attn. Special Sales Department, Phone: 1-800-221-2647.

Zebra and the Z logo Reg. U.S. Pat. & TM Off.

First Printing: October 2001
10 9 8 7 6 5 4 3 2 1

Printed in the United States of America

For Barb, Dixie, Diane and Diann, Laurie, Paulette and Wendy, the sisters of my heart without whom this wouldn't have been possible.

One

It was worse than she expected—he was not only young, he was handsome. Devastatingly so. Eleanor stood in the doorway to the drawing room, her hand cold on the brass doorknob. She could not force herself to step into the room where her parents—Lord and Lady Rushton—and her husband-to-be waited. Oh, she could not marry him. Not him. For he would never be happy with her.

No one in the room had yet noticed her entrance, but then the drawing room—the finest room in the house—was a cavern of a place, with the chairs and fireplace at one end and the doors at the other. The room took up the entire front of the house, overlooking Berkley Square. Faint light drifted in from behind the gold velvet curtains that stretched from plastered ceiling to polished floor. She looked down the distance, the windows to her right and portraits of intimidating ancestors to her left, and wished herself anywhere else.

She had always dreaded this place, with its stiff furniture, its cold drafts, and the demanding expectations that its use placed on her. Small as she was, she disappeared in this room. Elizabeth had always teased that it was the print muslin dresses in fashion which made every young lady appear far too similar to the surrounding wallpaper. Eleanor had laughed, but she also noted that the tall, sophisticated Elizabeth—even in sprig muslin—never could be called a wallflower. No, it was not Eleanor's dress which made her a person whom gentlemen looked past and ladies glanced at with little interest. Not in this room, nor in any other.

She was simply not a remarkable person.

For the most part, Eleanor had found it a relief to be so overlooked. She liked to overhear the gossip and observe the follies of those deeply involved in their lives. She liked being a spectator. It was so much . . . safer.

Only today she was to be put firmly into the center of everything. Today, she was to become engaged. Her parents had arranged everything with Lord Staines. This meeting was merely to confirm that she and her husband-to-be did not take an unreasonable dislike to each other.

But Eleanor knew already that she was no match for this gentleman—the heir to an earldom, and a handsome one at that.

He had golden hair, a thick cap of it that gleamed in the weak November sunlight that slanted in to pull a fair halo from his head. The shining strands lay in casual, curling disorder. *How on earth does he keep his hat from flattening it?* Eleanor thought. Self-conscious of her own appearance, she reached up to touch her own bonnet-flattened brown curls.

His dark blue coat stretched broad over his shoulders and nipped in at his waist, and hung open to show a yellow waistcoat. He did not seem vain, for his cravat was neatly tied but not with great flourish, and his shirt-points reached no higher than his square, firm chin.

His buckskin breeches formed a second skin over long, muscular legs. He stood a shade taller than her own father—Eleanor knew she would forever be craning to look up at him. Would he also step on her feet with his much larger ones when they danced? Would they dance? And what would it be like to have his so very much larger hands on her?

A treacherous heat flashed across her skin, and she looked down to hide it. She was a lady, and ladies were not supposed to think about a gentleman's hands upon their person. But no one looked at her to see the longing that she knew must be apparent on her face. And why should anyone glance at her, when he was so much easier on the eyes?

She looked up again.

He had his profile towards her, and she noted the perfectly straight nose, the clean jaw line, the arch of golden eyebrows, which rose arrogantly over eyes as blue as a perfect summer sky.

Her heart sank into her stomach. He needed a tall, dark beauty on his arm to make a striking contrast, or a golden-haired nymph who would match his own burnished looks. He did not need a brown mouse such as her. He must have wanted Elizabeth, really.

Then her mother looked up, smiled and rose, calling out, "Ah, Eleanor, come and meet Lord Staines, my child."

Eleanor tried to smile, but her face seemed unable to hold any expression and she could only pray that her eyes did not—as Emma often said they did—look as large as a frightened owl's. She turned to shut the door behind her, using that instant to pull in a breath and smooth the front of her best sprig muslin gown. Oh, how he must regret that he had ever allowed his father—and hers—to make this match.

Turning, she came into the room, trying to glide as Evelyn—the youngest of them all at fourteen—could already manage. Eleanor's own bouncing step had been the bane of their governess, despite every effort Eleanor made to control herself. Her father had never understood it and had always complained that it came from her striding about the countryside so much, but even after a season in London, Eleanor could not seem to manage a smooth, delicate step. She had to take long steps simply to keep up with everyone else.

However, even with her stride, it seemed to take years to reach the small group gathered beside the fire. When she did, she did not know where to put her hands or if she should sit or stand, so she bobbed a curtsy and then shot a terrified glance at her mother.

Her mother's eyes glowed with sympathy, but her expression also held its usual touch of exasperation, and Eleanor could almost hear her mother sigh that long-echoed phrase, *"Oh, Eleanor, what ever will become of you?"*

Instead of speaking the words aloud, her mother smiled until it strained her face and then said, "Lord Staines, may I present my second daughter, Miss Eleanor."

His lordship bowed and said nothing, and his sky-blue eyes glanced at her and away. Obviously, he was not delighted.

Eleanor smoothed her damp palms along the sides of her gown and struggled to think of something clever to say—something that might spark some life into his eyes. Something that might actually make him really look at her. Elizabeth, as the eldest, rightly held the title Miss Glover, and Eleanor wished now that she could be introduced as such. It would make her feel so much more adult to be Miss Glover, not Miss Eleanor.

Her silence earned a frown from her father and a small, distressed sigh from her mother.

"How do you do?" Eleanor finally managed, grimacing inside at how vapid she sounded. Now he would think her hen-witted as well as plain. It was such a shame that burning mortification could not actually kill one, as one so often wished it could.

Eleanor's father smoothed his graying side-whiskers with a finger and then tugged his waistcoat down over his thickening stomach. "Yes, well, we'll leave you to it, Staines. Come along, Evangeline."

Alarm shot through Eleanor as her father moved to escort her mother from the room. She sent a stricken glance to her mother, but that lady merely offered another of her encouraging smiles and then let her husband bear her away.

When the heavy door clicked shut, Eleanor fixed her stare on Lord Staines's boots and listened to the soft hiss from the coal fire. *How amazing,* she thought, heart hammering and mouth dry. *I can see my reflection in his boots. Mine are never so shiny. Doesn't he ever step in mud?*

"Miss Eleanor?"

Startled at his voice, she risked a glance at him. The sight of him, perfect and handsome, stopped her spinning mind and for an instant she could only stare at him, her breath caught in her chest and a warm tingle on her skin.

Reality intruded in a small voice that whispered, *You have nothing to interest the likes of him—save for a large dowry and a well-connected family.* He had chosen her only because of the ties between their families. She must accept that.

"Miss Eleanor," he began again, and then he raked a hand through his golden hair and turned aside. She heard him mutter something unsuitable for a lady to hear, so she pretended not to have heard.

Sudden impatience flared in her. Was he going to mutter her name all afternoon and hedge his way around this whole matter? Now that he had seen her, he must be wishing for an escape. Well, she would offer him one.

She sought at first to find some soft words to hint him away, but then, with her tone far too aggressive for any young lady, she blurted out, "You don't have to do this."

He looked at her. Really looked at her, and her heart sank even lower, because the fire smoldering in his eyes came from pure irritation.

"I am quite aware of what I am doing. Or is this your

way of saying you find my . . ." His chin lifted. His eyes narrowed. ". . . my reputation not to your taste?"

She opened her mouth to tell him that was it, exactly.

Like anyone in London, she had heard the stories. How could any man so sinfully handsome not have left a trail of broken hearts behind him? He was not quite a rake, but she strongly suspected it wasn't from not trying. However, he was young, and he had a title. Eleanor could not imagine that any of those elderly ladies who set Society's rules—and who chose the acceptable guest lists—would ever really brand this man too wild for the polite world and cast him out, like Lucifer thrown from the pearly gates. Not unless he did something really, really awful.

But she had heard enough stories over the past few months, during the spring and through summer, to know that some thought him fast. Some said he'd had his heart broken by another lady. Others whispered that any lady would be a fool to fall in love with such a reckless fellow.

And I am far too wise to be so foolish, Eleanor told herself.

So she opened her mouth to lie to him and tell him that she did object to his reputation. But, as it happened any time she tried to lie, the truth tumbled out before she could stop it.

"I don't think . . . I mean, you're not . . . well, it's just that I know you're supposed to offer for one of us, and with Elizabeth taken and me the next oldest, I . . ."

"I must marry someone," he interrupted, scowling at her, as if irritated by this delay to whatever other plans he had had for the afternoon.

"You must?" Eleanor repeated, feeling very dull and stupid. "But why now?" *And why me?* she thought, but did not have the courage to say.

Impatience twisted his mouth. For an instant he hesitated, and then he said, "Because my father is dying and it is his wish to see me married before this year is done, and him with it."

Those blunt words took the breath out of her. He didn't even want her family connections, or her dowry. He simply wanted some . . . some female. And, of course, why should she—such a plain snip of a girl, such an obedient daughter—refuse him? Her nose tingled and her eyes blurred.

She looked down at the carpet again. She would never forget its rose pattern. Nor would she forget the faint pine scent of his cologne, which tickled her nose with its pleasant difference from everything else she had ever known. And she would never forget how awful he had just made her feel.

How stupid. Of course he had to marry. And of course he would think her the type who could not refuse him, for she did not have it within her to inspire love in a man. His offer was the best she could ever hope for. Of course she must accept.

She wanted to cry.

"I see," she said, mumbling the words, because she really did see all too clearly how it was.

He went on, his voice gruff and a little daunting. "We're to marry at Westerley as soon as they've finished calling the banns. My father can't travel, so your family must come there, and will stay over Christmas. Afterwards . . . well, I've discussed the settlements with your father, and he's pleased. You'll have a London house, as well as apartments at Westerly. And . . ." He hesitated the merest second, and Eleanor wondered what to make of that break in this terrifying description of her future. "I expect you'll be a countess before too long."

"I don't want to be a countess," she muttered to the floor, unexpected rebellion rising inside her.

"What's that?" he asked, his voice sharp.

She looked up. Such a mistake. She met the blue eyes,

wary now and stormy, and words disappeared from her mind and her tongue. She fell into those eyes, and suddenly she knew how any lady could be too foolish when it came to him, for she wanted to do something to coax a smile from him, to thaw the sudden ice in his glance.

"Dammit, Eleanor, we might as well get this straight from the start."

She didn't wince at his swearing, though she knew that a well-bred girl such as herself ought to at least gasp at his language. However, he looked to be in such a temper that he had not even realized what he had said, and she thought it wiser not to pour oil on his fire by bringing it to his attention.

"Your father says you're a sensible girl," he went on, his words raspy and rapid. "I need a marriage, and I would rather get myself a sensible agreement with a sensible girl. Now, I know da—dashed well I don't need to make good on that silly pact my father made with yours to have one of his sons marry a Glover, but if it gives him some satisfaction in his dying days, then I shall do it. I'd rather not pick one of your sisters—I've . . . well, let us just say that by what your father tells, you seem the most likely to be satisfied with an arranged marriage. So, do we have an agreement, or not?"

He stood glaring at her, his hands clenched at his sides and his expression almost daring her to decline. He sounded far too much like a man who always got what he wanted. However, the problem was that he really didn't want her. He simply wanted someone sensible. And he thought her sensible.

She stared at him, at those intense eyes, and things—not very sensible things—popped into her head. But he would never want to hear any of them from her. They were fleeting thoughts. Momentary indulgences of the fantasies that she had woven around how it would be someday when someone asked her to marry him. They danced through her mind like dust motes in sunlight, mere glimmers of undefined longing that vanished before she could wrap words around them.

This was nothing like anything she had ever imagined. This was her choice. Take him, or send him away to find a truly sensible woman? Only she did not want to send him away.

It was his eyes, she decided. Or rather, it was what she had glimpsed for an instant deep within those eyes, lurking like some fabulous beast at the bottom of a crystal lake.

All her life, she had been drawn to wounded creatures. She had rescued rabbits from poachers' traps, had lured stray dogs into following her home, and had raised orphaned kittens. Over the years, her reputation at her father's estate had spread, and they'd even had three babies left on the steps, much to her parents' dismay. But her parents had allowed her her charities, for it was the one thing she had always turned obstinate about. It was a womanly virtue, after all.

So they had allowed her to nurse her animals, and to find homes for the unwanted babies, and to keep the dogs at their country estate in the Lake District.

It seemed she now had a new rescue—or did she?

Why, after all, would Lord Staines, future earl that he was, have that look of a wounded, wild thing, all bristly in case she should think him helpless, and ready to snap out at anyone or anything?

A shiver chased up her arms and down her spine. The muslin gown, with its high collar, seemed suddenly too thin for this room. Her nose twitched with an itch, but she did not rub it.

Her mother had warned that her soft heart would one day be her undoing. That day seemed to have come.

Only, had she been mistaken about that haunted look?

"Well?" he demanded, startling her from her thoughts. "I would have your answer today."

Stubborn pride rose in her. Leaning back a little, she looked him straight in the eye. "You would? Well, I would like to know what do I get from this agreement?"

For an instant, he held quite still. She wanted to slap a hand over her mouth for letting her thoughts leap out unchecked. Those blue eyes frosted with icy fire, and she knew she ought to beg his pardon, only she did not have that much courage.

Then the corner of his mouth crooked.

"You mean, I take it, that you want something other than a title, my name, and endowment of all my worldly goods?"

It sounded greedy when he put it that way. A flush warmed her cheeks, but she held her ground. "You said you wanted someone sensible. How sensible would it be to agree to something when I do not know if I shall get out of it what I want?"

Light danced in his eyes, and the expression set her heart thudding so hard she thought he must hear it. *Oh, dear.* She felt as if she had stepped out on a slim and terribly fragile branch. But that was silly. She had given up tree-climbing years ago.

With a lift of one eyebrow, he regarded her. Then he gave a small nod. "Very well, my sensible miss. What do you want?"

The question sent a small, panicked shock through her. Her mind blanked. *Oh, heavens, what?*

She turned away, groping for something to say. She had thought that he would make her an offer. Only he had turned the tables utterly on her. He really was quite infuriating.

Stalling for time, she walked to a side table. There, on the silver platter that the butler must have brought in to her parents, lay his card with small black print on the white laid cardstock.

Geoffrey F. Westerley, Lord Staines

Inspiration struck.

She picked up the card and turned to him, her skin cold. Well, now he would either give a sharp laugh and walk out—and, she told herself firmly, she would be much better off if he did—or . . . or . . .

Her voice shook a little and she had to clear her throat. And then she said, "I have heard that some gentlemen offer a *carte blanche* to some . . . ladies? Not the ones they wish to marry, but to the other sort."

Both golden brows lifted and he looked down that long, straight nose of his from his rather awesome height. "What of it?" he asked, his tone bleak enough to send shivers across the back of her bare arms.

She hesitated only a moment, preparing herself for his anger. Then she said, "I want *carte blanche* to name what I wish from this arrangement."

Geoffrey stared at the slip of a girl before him. This was not going the way he had planned, and irritation flared into snarling anger that she wasn't acting her part. Why did she not drop a meek curtsy, say yes, and let them both get on with it? Her parents had talked of her as if she knew her duty and her manners.

Damnation.

But then the humor of it slipped under his guard and began to unravel his dark mood like a teasing jester.

He had always had the most damnable luck when it came to affairs of the heart. Why should that change now? And, by God, she was more than sensible to make certain she got what she wanted out of this bargain.

Wary, he eyed the blank card. Her slim hand held it firm and fast. She had nerve, at least. And nice hands, with tapering fingers and smooth, round nails. He glanced up at her face. She also had a stubborn chin. It stood out in contrast to those doe-brown eyes which seemed to dominate her face. Which should he heed more—those soft eyes or that square chin?

"Well, Lord Staines?" she asked again, the faintest tremor betraying that she was not as confident as she seemed.

Oh, devil take this bit of Eve. What did she really want of him? There seemed but one way to find out.

"Very well. Write what you want and give it to me at Westerley. You may have what you will from me for your bride gift as well as a Christmas gift, so I will have back that card before we wed."

She stuck out her hand to him.

He almost laughed at the absurdity of it. What a way to propose and take a bride, with a handshake and a bargain. Still, he had tried it once before in a more conventional sense, with confessions of devoted love and passionate embraces, and what a nightmare that had ended.

Still, it rankled him that she seemed so in control. For an instant, that devil inside him tempted him to sweep her into his arms—she'd tuck neatly into his grip, small as she was—and kiss her light-headed. It would give him infinite satisfaction to do so, and then to demand of her if she were still willing to make a bargain with him. Only, devil take it, he needed a wife. And he needed one now. He could not afford to frighten a second one off.

So he took her slim hand in his and gave it a firm shake. She had soft hands, but strong, and she wore no rings. At least she did not seem to be a vain, rapacious sort of female. She probably wouldn't demand gems or riches.

What would she ask for?

"Then we have an understanding," he said, letting go

of her, and folding his own hands behind his back. Lord, what should he do now? Ask about the weather? About what ball she had attended last night?

He rocked on his heels a moment and watched her stare down at the blank card in her hand.

Oh, devil take it!

"Well, good-day then." He gave a quick bow and started for the door, unable to keep his long stride from betraying his need to escape.

Her voice, small and light as a bird's song, stopped him at the door. "And will I see you tonight, Lord Staines, at Lady Farquar's autumn ball?"

Two

He turned and stared down the length of the room. She looked even more tiny—a slip of a thing with brown curls, brown eyes, and a white gown with flowery bits strewn over it, which covered her from neck to toe. What the devil was he doing, asking to marry such a child? Still, that was what he'd heard was best. Marry 'em young, before they learned to expect anything. And she was not as young as Cynthia had been.

His mind skirted away from that thought.

He gave her another bow. "Do you wish me to come?"

Even from the distance across the room, he saw the sudden panic in her eyes. "That's not what I want to write on the card. That's not my one wish."

He started to smile, then had to wipe the expression from his face. He did not want her to think he was laughing at her, for it was himself that he found amusing. She made him sound like some sort of magical wizard, and nothing could be further from the truth. "A bride-to-be may also make requests of her husband. I shall be honored to escort you."

And then he turned and fled before she could ask anything else of him.

* * *

"If you're trying to get drunk, you're doing a damn bad job of it." Lounging in his chair, Patrick Westerley regarded his brother over the glass in his hand.

Geoff glanced around at the long faces gathered in this dim corner of White's gaming club and wished that he was drunk. This early in the evening few gentlemen had yet to wend their way to the exclusive club on St. James's Street. He and his brothers had this corner to themselves. What had he been thinking of to try and celebrate this blasted betrothal in his current ill-humor?

Trying to force a lighter mood into his soul and a wry tone into his voice, he gave back a twisted smile. "If I were trying, I would not have ordered champagne. This is a celebration, damn it, now are you going to drink to my wedded bliss or not?"

"Geoff, old fellow, you're not marrying for love, so I don't see how bliss enters into it. Shall we drink to a long life instead?" Andrew asked, his voice as dry as the champagne in his glass. Two years younger than Geoffrey, he looked like a man intended for a career in the Church— soberly dressed, with his slender form and his serious manner. However, the mischief in his blue-green eyes rather spoilt the full effect of a dark-clad clergyman.

"No, let's drink to a sensible agreement for our sensible brother," Patrick said, raising his glass again, his voice drawling and teasing.

Geoff regarded his brothers with unease. Patrick, the youngest of them at twenty-three, looked most like their late mother. He was the sturdiest of them all, and the dark one of the family, with only a shading of gold in his brown hair. He had, however, the straight Westerley nose and the same height as his fair-headed brothers. He also had the family blue eyes, and the devil's own light in them when he intended trouble. Right now, Geoff could see the warning glints and knew his brother intended to roast him unmercifully. He should have let them read the damn announcement in the paper, like the rest of the world.

"And what do you think I should have done, instead?" Geoff demanded, wishing he did not feel so petulant about all this. Damn it, why couldn't he laugh about it with them? Perhaps because it was his own future being ridiculed. "Should I wait another decade or two, perhaps? I'm twenty-eight, and I ought to know . . ."

"Exactly what's in your stubborn head, and not much more," Andrew said, interrupting. He poured the rest of the champagne from the dark glass bottle into the crystal goblets and lifted a narrow hand for the waiter to bring more of the smuggled French wine to them. "But this is hardly the occasion to brawl about it."

Geoff took up his glass and stared into the dissipating bubbles. A brawl would suit him just now. However, one was not supposed to celebrate an engagement with a fight. What the devil was that girl planning to write on that card, anyway? She'd have her own house. Servants. Money. What else could she want? His fidelity? His love? Scowling, he tossed back his champagne. She would do better to ask for all the stars in heaven.

"Are you certain you must go through with it, Geoff?" Andrew asked, his expression sober now and worry tugging his long face into a frown. "The old man's been on his death bed before."

"Before?" Patrick gave a rude snort. "He has had more dying moments than Kean's run of Hamlet. He sent me at least twenty letters at Oxford, all of them urging me to take my degree with honors before he turned up his toes. And fat lot of good any honors ever done me in the Home Office."

Patrick fell to grumbling into his drink, muttering about his stalled political career.

Geoff hadn't wanted to tell them, but now he decided

the moment had come. They would know the truth of it soon enough.

"This time it's different," he said, his tone flat. "This time Ibbottson wrote me."

The others looked at him, their expressions arrested, but Geoff could see that their thoughts now mirrored what had been his own overwhelmed shock when he had read that letter. Dr. Ibbottson had been treating the Earl of Herndon, and his family, for twenty years. A heavy-set, blunt-spoken man, Ibbottson had never once indulged their father's attempts to use his forever failing health to rule his sons' lives. But if Ibbottson had written that the earl had little time left, well then. . . .

Silence descended on the trio. From the other room the rattle of dice in a dice box could be heard. It sounded a damn death rattle.

For Geoffrey, the champagne soured in his mouth. He would be married in less than a month, at Christmas time, the season of joy and goodwill to all, and then he was likely to see his father buried shortly thereafter. A joyous season indeed, he thought, the pulse beating hard in his clenched jaw. He filled his glass from the fresh bottle set down by a waiter, and then threw back the cold, bubbling liquid. Its faint bitterness echoed the mix of regret that already lay inside him.

Well, that Glover girl would certainly earn whatever it was that she wanted from him. She'd earn it all right, if she married him.

Uneasily, he wondered if she might cry off when it came to the sticking point. He doubted she would, not if she were really the sensible creature he had been told she was. But he'd have to make damn sure she didn't learn the truth about him before they were properly shackled. After all, even a sensible woman might not care to marry a man who had no heart.

"Geoffrey?"

He glanced up to see Andrew staring at him as if expecting an answer.

"Come out of your thoughts and decide. Do you have Patrick for your groomsman, or me? And don't ask me to perform the rites, for it'll have to be the new vicar—what's his name, Cleverly . . . Cheesley. . . ."

"Cheeverly," Geoffrey said, almost spitting out the word.

Andrew and Patrick exchanged a dark look. Then Andrew sat up and forced a brighter tone. "Yes, well, Cheesley or whatever will have to do it up since I've yet to take my orders. But I don't think your bride will mind."

"Don't know about that," Patrick said. "Seems to me, you give a female a wedding and all of a sudden they've an opinion on every detail of your life. Happened to poor Smyth-Winston when he married that Telford chit. She had him jumping through hoops for her. Taking her everywhere. Buying her everything."

"Oh, damn," Geoff muttered, suddenly recalling he had indeed made a promise to take his intended somewhere. He glanced down at his morning clothes, in which he had made his proposal and then wandered about London for far too long. They were not the formal breeches and coat he would need to attend any sort of do.

He swore again, then put down his glass and rose. "Your pardon, but I must go."

"Go? Go where?" Patrick asked, startled.

Geoff paused, a cynical smile on his lips. "I have a hoop to jump through."

Andrew and Patrick watched their elder brother stride across the deep carpets and out the portal of White's, then Andrew gave a deep sigh. "Ten to one this doesn't turn out well."

Patrick's scowl deepened, and a lock of dark hair fell across his forehead, making him look like a brooding poet. "It can't end like last time. Geoff may not say much about it, but I'm not having him cut up like that again. And you heard him when he spoke that fellow's name."

Andrew let out a sigh. "Yes, I'd hoped he'd have it out of his system by now. But I am not certain what we can do about any of this. Geoff won't thank us for any interference. He's too accustomed to being the capable elder brother."

Patrick studied the bubbles in his glass a moment, then looked up, his mouth set and the look in his eyes stubborn. "Yes, he is. But if we don't do something, I'll lay you ten to one that Geoff makes a mull of this with that temper of his. You know that must be what happened last time."

Stirring in his chair, Andrew shot an uneasy glance at his brother. "I know no such thing. And neither do you. But you are right on one account. We'd best keep an eye on the proceedings." He tossed back his champagne and then smiled. "So who is on guard duty tonight?"

It took three tours of the Farquar's ballroom for Geoffrey to find his quarry.

He had started to think that Lord and Lady Rushton had brought their daughters and taken them away again when he finally spotted her, for the rooms were not that thick with company. How could they be on a chilly November night, with so many already fled from London?

Fox hunting had begun, and so had pheasant season. Society bucks had fled either to the hunt field, taking their mistresses with them, or to the shooting boxes on their country estates. A few peers had stayed to attend to Parliament, but when that business was done, they, like the rest of the decent world, would abandon London, leaving its coal-yellowed skies to the merchants and the unfashionable until next spring came and the weather improved again. Christmas was the season for country parties and pleasant entertainment at tidy, warm estates.

However, even a London thin of company was still a place where the world craved its entertainment. Events had to be held for gossip to spread and scandal to form. Hence the Farquar's ball.

It occurred suddenly to Geoffrey that Lady Rushton would want to hold an engagement ball. He did not want to linger in London, but perhaps his bride-to-be and her family wanted to make the most of her success. She would probably want to shop, as well, for bride things and such, although he had no clear idea, he realized, just what she might want for her trousseau. Bride clothes had not occupied his mind the last time he had proposed.

Scowling at that thought, he pulled his attention back to his current situation and away from useless, ruined desires.

The two Miss Glovers, Elizabeth and the younger Eleanor, sat together near the far wall. As he watched, a man in military garb came up to them, bowed over the blushing Elizabeth's hand and took her away for a dance, leaving Eleanor to herself. Without company, Eleanor folded her hands in her lap, and Geoffrey watched her make herself disappear.

It was actually quite an amazing process, involving more not-doing than doing. Head up, she became quite still, and soon seemed to become part of the furnishings. When two gossiping old ladies took the seats next to her, Eleanor's lips quivered once or twice, but she said nothing and did not look at the gossips. He felt quite certain, however, that this was how she had acquired her knowledge of men who gave scandalous women a *carte blanche*.

Folding his arms, Geoff leaned against the wall near a tapestry and set to watching his betrothed. He ought to ask her to dance, and so he would—eventually. For now, he only wanted to study her, to try and see beneath that calm exterior which she presented to the world.

It had been a stupid thing to agree so blindly to her

condition of naming what she wanted from a marriage. He had only wanted to be done with the matter, to have it over and fixed so that he could not change his mind. He had needed a bride, and now he had one. But what sort of woman was she that she could seem so meek and yet make such a nearly scandalous demand of him?

Carte blanche, indeed!

And then his lips twitched at the memory of that scene. He could not think of any other miss who would have made such a shocking request. No, usually, they were falling over themselves to charm the heir to an earldom.

Eyes narrowing, he studied his bride-to-be. She sat so still, her head down, not looking at anyone. Not talking. She looked far too shy for any man's taste, and an uneasy doubt made him wonder if he had chosen badly. His future countess would have certain public duties, after all.

And then the image of her with her chin up and her hand out as she asked him for a *carte blanche* stirred in his thoughts again, teasing him with the same question.

What did she want?

As he watched, her lips curved into a secret smile. She kept her stare focused on the tips of her white satin slippers, but that smile had his fingers twitching with the desire to tip up that stubborn chin so he could see what secret amusement lay hidden in those infernally downcast eyes.

What was she smiling at? Gossip? Some secret thoughts?

Had he gotten himself some clever female who hid unreasonable desires in her heart? Was she thinking up some sensible request to make, or would she ask for romantic nonsense?

Pushing away from the wall, he straightened. Damn it all, he was going to have to find out just what sort of female he had gotten himself here. And if she had any quixotic notions about him, he would just have to make certain he eliminated those from her head before they were bound together as man and wife. At least that was one thing he was good at. He knew how to make a lady cry, and how to destroy her faith in him forever.

Eleanor sat with her eyes downcast as she listened to an utterly unsuitable story of how Lady Charlotte Wellesley had eloped with Lord Paget this past spring. The lady had left her husband and four children for the gallant cavalry officer. He, in turn, had been drawn by love to abandon a cheating wife. It all sounded terribly improper, and the gossiping ladies had nothing but criticism for the couple. But wistful delight curled into Eleanor.

How wonderful to love and be loved so passionately that nothing else mattered.

She let out a small sigh, and then became aware that a pair of gentlemen's evening slippers had moved into her view. Her stare traveled up from those black slippers, over strong calves encased in white, clocked stockings, over buff satin breeches that lay smooth over muscular legs, to a gold shot brocade waistcoat and a dark green evening coat, and then to the impassive face of Lord Staines.

Her mouth dried and her heart thudded into her throat, leaving her unable to speak.

He took her breath away, with those burnished locks and the heart-stopping perfection of his face. But he regarded her without fire or flash in eyes as chilly as winter ice.

She smiled and stammered out a good evening.

With a short bow, he held out his hand. "May I have this dance?"

Startled, she glanced around herself. No one ever asked her to dance. And then she remembered that, of course, he would have to ask her. They were to be married, after all.

Putting her gloved hand in his, she rose. He held her hand firmly, but he kept a polite distance between them.

Remembering all the lessons she'd had with the dancing master this past season, she kept her stare fixed not on her feet—as she longed to—but on the glinting emerald tucked into the folds of his perfect, white cravat. She had to look somewhere, and she did not trust herself to stare into his face and remain the sensible girl that he expected.

The small orchestra engaged for the evening played the opening bars to the dance. Lord Staines bowed, she curtsied, and they moved into the steps. The dance had them separate, and then they came together and he took her hands to turn her.

"Is this punishment for my being late?" he asked.

Her gaze flew to his face, but those devastating blue eyes regarded her only with slight curiosity.

"I beg your pardon," she said. "I . . . I was just minding my steps."

The dance separated them again—thankfully—and when they came together, he leaned closer. "Are the steps more interesting than I am?"

Her glance shot back up again to his face. This time she glimpsed a spark of devilment in his eyes. She tensed. She was done for if he started flirting with her. She was not like Emma. If he started to tease her, she might fall under the spell of his charm, and that would be a fatal mistake in what was only a marriage of convenience. No, she must honestly be sensible about this.

The dance forced them apart and Geoff cursed himself for thinking a country dance any place for conversation. He felt like a damn jack-in-the-box, popping up at odd moments to say something to her, and then popping away before she answered. However, he had seen the flare of panic in her eyes when he had teased her about minding her steps. He felt as if he had kicked a kitten. He wanted at once to say something to reassure her, but the movement in the dance took him away.

When they met again as partners, she took his hands

for another turn. With a smile fixed in place, she said, "It is my company that is not very good, I fear."

He had been thinking just that, but her admission—made in such a soft, wrenching voice—instantly had him wanting to deny any such thing.

They reached the end of the line of dancers and had to stand out, and at last he could talk to her. And he decided that a new approach was needed. Something more direct, for they had dealt with each other better than this when they had both spoken plainly this morning.

"Why do you think you are not good company?" he asked.

She glanced up at him, and he saw her thoughts turning behind those wide brown eyes. *Well, it is not a dull mind that keeps her silent.* And his shoulders relaxed a little. Like his father, he did not suffer fools well, and he had not even realized until now how unbearable it would be to be shackled to a dull woman.

Hesitating over her words, she wet her lips, and then said, "Good company in London seems to consist of either making cutting comments about others, or smiling stupidly and giggling at everything a gentleman says. I don't do either."

Her answer amused him. She had described the catty ladies and the simpering misses that he knew all too well. "Your smile is intriguing, Miss Eleanor. Quite intriguing. In fact, I wonder what it is that makes you smile? It is not, I gather, a cutting comment?"

He had stepped closer as he spoke, and now fear sparked at the back of her eyes. Cursing himself, he stepped away at once. He must remember to keep himself in check. He would not let that side of himself out again. Not with a lady at least. He did not want her knowing what sort of monster courted her.

The dance shifted, pulling them back into the line.

Allowing her to keep her stare focused on his chest, he

tried not to feel like such a bloody idiot. He had presumed too much. In that brief moment of companionship, he had acted as if they knew each other, when in fact they were utter strangers. No wonder she looked at him with alarm.

This was not going well, he thought, angry with himself for already making such a botch of it.

At last the dance ended. Eleanor made her curtsy and then stood there, wondering what she ought to do. Did she ask him to take her back to her parents? Or would he do that on his own? He looked so terrifying, so perfect and terrifying. She did not know what to do with him.

Normally, the very few gentlemen she danced with were friends of her fathers. Older men who joked with her and made her forget her nervousness. They did not have intense blue eyes. They did not have powerful shoulders. And the touch of their gloved hands on hers did not make her stomach flutter. For an instant, when Lord Staines had stepped close to her, she had felt that sweep of intense male virility close around her, and she had frozen.

Would he touch more than her hand? She had wanted him to, and the strength of that desire shocked and frightened her.

She had been grateful when he stepped away—but she had almost reached out her hand to him to make him come back to her.

Oh, you stupid girl. He wants a sensible bride, not some half-infatuated ninny!

Straightening, she swallowed the dryness in her mouth and smiled at him. "Thank you for the dance."

He took her hand and started to lead her off the floor, but then the first notes of a lively jig sounded. She glanced over her shoulder at the other dancers starting to assemble—the ladies with eager faces, the laughing gentlemen. Oh, how much fun they were having, she thought, the smile already forming on her lips for their pleasure.

When she turned back, she found Lord Staines staring

down at her, his eyes narrowed and his look measuring. She blushed, glanced down, but then looked up again. She would not have him thinking that she found the floor more interesting than him.

The mischief glinted again in his eyes, as irresistible as fairy gold. "Shall we shock the gossips and dance a second time in a row?"

"We shall have everyone talking. It is just not done, you know."

He grinned. "It's past time London noticed you, Miss Eleanor Glover."

And then he led her into the fast-paced jig.

The dance gave her no time and no breath for talk. But Eleanor needed neither. With him smiling at her and dancing her up and down the line, she needed nothing. The world whirled past in bright music and sweet colors, and she even allowed herself to laugh. She threw back her head and let the happiness out for the world to see. She had never danced like this. Not even at home with her sisters.

It ended before she was ready. The musicians struck the last chord, drawing it out for the dancers to pay honors to their partners. But the music still hummed in her—and so did a rare delight.

He led her from the dance floor, taking her all the way to the sidelines this time. And she turned to him, thinking that now she could talk to him. After all, how could anyone feel shy with someone after being spun about. But the smiling man she had danced with was gone.

He was looking elsewhere, and she followed his gaze to see him staring at a man who must be his brother, for the straight nose and tall, handsome form was so like him. The man gave a nod to Lord Staines, who returned the greeting with a gesture.

Turning to her, polite and distant, the perfect gentleman, he gave her a bow. "Thank you for the dances, Miss Eleanor."

Then he was gone.

It was like stepping from sunshine into deep shade. She blinked and glanced about her. The ladies around her whispered and gossiped behind their fans—probably about her having danced twice with the same man. With the reckless Lord Staines, in fact. Gentlemen eyed her, their stares now assessing, as if seeking what it was that had attracted Staines's attention. Blood rushed into her cheeks in a fierce heat. Too conscious of being in the center of things, the panic caught in her chest.

Taking deep breaths, she forced herself to walk back to her chair, her back straight, her face on fire. And she knew suddenly that the biggest danger before her was that it would be all too easy to fall in love with her husband-to-be.

Only would that really be so awful?

She glanced over to him, to the fine line of his back which he presented to the room. Already, some other lady—beautiful and dark, wearing diamonds and a gown cut to reveal almost everything—had come up to him. She leaned on his arm to whisper something in his ear and he turned and leaned closer to her. A twisted smile curved his lips, and a dangerous light glittered in his eyes.

Oh, yes, it would be awful to love him. Awful and wonderful, and heart-breaking.

Eleanor folded her hands tight together on her lap, and wondered what Lord Staines would do if she simply wrote on the back of his cards—*I want your heart.*

Of course, she would not. She could not. She'd die if she did so and he laughed—and of course he would, for such words were ludicrous coming from a mouse of a girl such as her.

But if she didn't write that, what was she to write?

Three

"So, what did he say? And what did you say? And what did he say in answer to your having asked?" Emma asked, sounding more as she had at thirteen than the sophisticated sixteen she had recently become.

"You sound such a magpie," Elizabeth scolded, and then turned back to Eleanor. "But when he proposed, did you really ask for a . . . a . . ."

"A *carte blanche*," Evelyn said, now laying upside down on the sofa in what had once been the nursery. The room, with its scarred floor, faded carpets, and worn green velvet draperies, seemed to Eleanor, at the moment, to be the safest of havens.

For Eleanor, it held both treasured toys and memories: Poor Anne Boleyn, who had been so named after Evelyn somehow lost the doll's head; George, the much tattered hobby-horse, who had been christened for the uncle who presented him one Christmas, and whose color had changed to suit each girl in turn. The walls held their youthful efforts in watercolors and embroidery, including Emma's dreadful still-life paintings, and Elizabeth's colorful but crooked needlepoint homilies. During all the years that the girls had come to London with their parents, even before they stepped into society, this had been their home from home.

Eleanor let out a sigh. All too soon this would no longer be her home. She would be married and moved elsewhere. The thought terrified her.

She had retreated that morning to the nursery to be with her sisters and ask their advice about her card, and about this marriage that loomed before her. Now she wondered if that had been such a wise thing, for they seemed more inclined to pelt her with questions than to offer any wisdom.

In response to Evelyn's pert answer about Eleanor having asked for a *carte blanche,* Elizabeth scolded, "You are not supposed to know such things!"

"Rubbish. I'm just not supposed to talk about them," Evelyn said, and then grinned. They all knew that Elizabeth's anger came out as soft as her words.

Eleanor regarded her sisters, her coming loss starting to weigh on her. Would she see them often after she married? Or would she live most of the year at Westerley? Well, if that happened, she would just have to invite them to stay, for she could not bear the thought of not seeing them.

Elizabeth, the eldest, was the beauty of the family, with her cloud of warm brown hair and her deep green eyes. But Emma, with her bright blue eyes, her infectious laugh and her plump curves, drew almost as many eyes as Elizabeth's quiet beauty. Even Evelyn, only fourteen and still in that age of being more legs and arms than anything else, seemed blessed with the promise of beauty in her dark hair and eyes.

Eleanor loved her sisters too well to begrudge them their gifts, but there were times she had wished that she was something more than their sensible Eleanor. Now she was to be that something more. She was to be Lady Staines. And she had that wretched blank card hanging over her. Why could she think of nothing to wish for from him?

"It is all true," she said. "And there is no getting out of it." She held out the copy of *The London Times* that she had pirated from her father's morning mail and pointed to the pertinent column. It had been nearly a week since her dances with Lord Staines at the Farquar's ball, but apparently that evening had not given his lordship second thoughts about sending in the notice that let the world know their plans.

She had seen little of his lordship, but that did not surprise her. Her days seemed full of shopping—hats to buy, and dresses, and linen, and china, and calling cards to order with her new title and direction. She had had so many fittings for so many dresses that she had begun to feel like a pin cushion.

Emma leaned over Elizabeth's shoulder, and even Evelyn sat up for a better look at the announcement, which made the engagement official to the world, and iron-clad, as far as Society was concerned. If Eleanor were to reject Lord Staines now, the world would brand her a foolish jilt, and she could not endure thrusting her family into such horrible scandal. Better to marry and live quietly in the country forever than that.

Lowering the paper, Elizabeth watched her sister with worry deepening the green in her eyes. "Oh, Ellie, I do wish you could marry for love, not just because you must marry someone."

"Love!" Evelyn wrinkled her nose. "Ellie doesn't need that. She's going to be a countess. Ellie, you should ask him for your own stable."

"But he must have a stable already, silly," Emma protested. She had just come out of the school room this year and more often than not forgot to act like a lady rather than a boisterous schoolgirl.

"That's not the same as having your own," Evelyn insisted, returning to her upside down position, with her long, dark brown hair hanging to the floor and her heels hooked over the back of the sofa.

Emma turned back to Eleanor, her expression serious as she strove for a superior sophistication that would put Evelyn in her place. "Ignore that child. You should ask him to be faithful and honor his vows to you."

Eleanor drew back, shocked. Over the past week, she had learned more of Lord Staines's reputation with the ladies—not respectable ladies, of course, but with those creatures who existed on the tattered edge of Society and whose business it was to give men pleasure. There was no one woman she knew of whose name had been linked with his. However, Eleanor had gone out of her way to listen to every conversation that concerned Lord Staines, and there seemed to have been a depressing list of light-skirts who had caught his eye over the past season.

"But what if I make him miserable with such a demand?" she said. "What an awful marriage we should have then."

Gracefully, Elizabeth rose. She took Emma's hand, and then urged Evelyn upright and ushered both girls from the room. "I wish to talk to Eleanor alone. Emma, why do you not go and read to mother, you know how she loves your voice, and . . ."

"I know, I know. I should be at my studies," Evelyn said, with a deep sigh and her heels dragging.

Reluctantly, both girls left, but as soon as the door had shut, it popped open again, and Evelyn poked her head in the doorway, her dark eyes sparkling. "Ask him for a black phaeton picked out in purple trim," she said, and then ducked out as Elizabeth shied a faded velvet pillow at the door.

"I hope you know that they only want the best for you," Elizabeth said, coming over to sit next to Eleanor.

Eleanor smiled as Elizabeth took her hand. "Of course I know. It's just . . . oh, Liz, I was so stupid to ask him for this *carte blanche.* Now I must ask him for something. And he will feel honor-bound to oblige me, no matter how it ultimately festers inside him. I thought I was being clever at the time, and that it would make him recant his offer. But I have put myself in a corner!"

And I want to ask him for something I haven't the nerve to ask for, she added silently. Not even to her sister could she confess the desire that had taken root inside her that she might ask him for just a little of his affection.

Elizabeth's eyes darkened, and a worried frown drew her eyebrows together. "I do wish, my dear, that you had waited to find someone who loves you."

Eleanor had to look down as she bit off the sharp words that she might have waited forever in that case. Elizabeth's face glowed with love, and the jab of jealousy twisting inside Eleanor shocked her. She, like Emma and Evelyn, had been so happy when Elizabeth had fallen in love with her Captain Singleton. Of course, they had taken it for granted that he would love her. Everyone loved Elizabeth. Who could not love such a sweet and kind and beautiful creature?

But now Eleanor feared that she would spoil Elizabeth's happiness with this loveless match she had made for herself, and with these silly notions that she had begun to indulge. She must get hold of herself, and simply stop daydreaming about Lord Staines as if he were some golden creature from a fairy story. She really must. She would be reasonable about this, and she would think up a nice, reasonable request. Perhaps she would ask for that stable, as Evelyn had advised.

"Just promise me one thing, Ellie," Elizabeth said, her voice unusually firm.

Eleanor looked up. "I will if I can."

"Please, make certain that you ask him for something you honestly do want. I cannot imagine that any man would care to find out his gift is not truly valued."

Blinking, Eleanor stared at her sister. She had not thought of this, but she saw at once that Elizabeth was exactly right. She could picture Lord Staines's eyes icing over if she trivialized her demand by asking for something inane—such as a stable. He would find out, too, if she asked for something that did not really matter to her. He was not a stupid man, and she was all too transparent with her emotions.

Eleanor looked down at the newspaper in her hands. She wet her lips, then pulled together her courage. "Do you think, then, that I should ask him for his . . ."

A knock on the door interrupted, and their mother swept in, all bustling smiles. "There you are. Emma said you were hiding up here. But you must hurry and change for we are to go out. And, Eleanor, you cannot wear that old gown. You must change quickly into that new fawn dress of yours."

"Change? But why? Where are we going?" Eleanor asked as her mother shepherded them out of the nursery. She glanced at Elizabeth, who could only stare back, a helpless sympathy in her eyes. Eleanor looked back at her mother.

Lady Rushton's smile took on a set look, and Eleanor shivered from a chill. That look always foretold something that was for the girls' best interest—whether they liked it or not.

Then her mother said, "Lord Staines has come to escort us shopping. And we must do our best to please him, and make him realize what a wonderful treasure he has gotten in our dear Eleanor."

Eleanor smiled weakly. She disliked shopping. All those choices. All those opportunities to choose wrong. And now she would have to make all the mistakes that she always made about selecting too strong a color and too garish a design under Lord Staines's all-too-uncomfortable stare.

* * *

"My God, I hope that child's not the one you're marrying. She looks an utter handful."

Geoff glanced over to the entrance of Lady Rushton's drawing room. He and Patrick stood near the fireplace at the far end of the room, and Patrick had spoken low enough so as not to have been heard by the girl who had just danced into the room, bobbed a curtsy and then darted out again with a giggle.

"That's not her," Geoff said, fretting his watch fob with his fingers. His cravat seemed ready to strangle him, and he wished that he had not thought of this idea to go shopping. With November now gone, however, and the days shortening to Christmas, it seemed an ideal way both to amuse the Glovers before they left London for Westerley, and to gain a better idea of Eleanor's intentions about that damn card by observing her tastes.

Then Patrick had offered to come along.

A simple shopping expedition had now become an outing that included Patrick, Lady Rushton, and two more of the Glover daughters. They would need a bloody wagon to haul them about if anyone else joined the fray. To add the final delight to the day, the windows showed a view of gathering clouds that hung low and heavy over London.

Rain and a parcel of chattering women. Just lovely.

The door opened again, and this time three young ladies came in with Lady Rushton. Geoff assumed that the child they had glimpsed must have been banished for her impertinence in showing herself. She had certainly been far too young to be seen outside the schoolroom.

As the ladies came forward, Geoff leaned closer to his brother. "Mine's the one in fawn. The invisible one."

Patrick glanced at him, eyebrows raised, but then Lady Rushton was upon them and introducing her offspring to Patrick.

Recognizing the tallest of the three as Miss Glover, Geoff studied the girl. Classically beautiful, he could admire her fine-spun golden-brown hair, her delicate features and her green eyes with dispassionate interest. In the other times he had met her, she had struck him as a sweet enough girl, who would never trouble any man overmuch.

Her sister, Emma, seemed a different proposition.

Clad in blue to match her eyes, Emma Glover came forward to make her curtsy, confident and smiling, her chin up and her assessing stare almost too bold. Pretty chit, Geoff judged, with an eye honed by his recent months of indulgence with the female form. All curves and mischievous smiles. He liked her at once for that pert stare of hers—the one that measured him up and almost dared him not to be good enough for her sister. But she was no more in his style than were her sisters, really. He had always preferred fair women. Fair and charming.

Like Cynthia.

He tried to banish that ghost, and forced his attention back to these ladies, to his sensible Miss Eleanor, and to Lady Rushton who was still rattling on, sounding too anxious to please.

Devil take her, what is she so worried about, Geoff wondered? Emma's possible misbehavior? Eleanor's being too withdrawn?

Geoff made the ladies known to his brother, and then some imp prompted him to ask, just to see what Lady Rushton would say, "But did we not see one more Glover daughter a moment ago? Are we to be denied her acquaintance?"

Flustered, Lady Rushton forced a stilted laugh. "Dear Evelyn. She so wanted to meet you, which is why she came in to see you, but she has her studies to finish."

A smile twitched at Geoff's lips, and he wondered if "Dear Evelyn" was now studying decorum, and writing a hundred times, "I will not introduce myself to gentlemen."

Lady Rushton went on with shopping plans, all the while seeking Geoff's approval for every possibility. The beginnings of boredom nibbled at him. It would be a dull afternoon if Lady Rushton was intent on treating him with all the awkward deference due his station.

The unpleasant sensation flashed through him that the woman's careful treatment of him smacked of his being a prize trout about to be netted. Immediately, an image of Lady Rushton, hip deep in water, a net in one hand and a pole in the other, flashed into his mind. His lips twitched and he cleared his throat to cover his smile. Awareness of being watched feathered across the back of his neck and he glanced to his right.

Eleanor's stare fell to the floor as soon as his gaze caught hers. He watched her, willing her to look up, wondering if she had caught his smile and what she made of it.

And then he could have sworn that the faintest answering smile teased her lips. Had the same thought crossed her mind? Or did she hug some other secret amusement close to her?

Before he could move next to her to ask, Miss Glover—Elizabeth—came forward to make small talk with him, Emma Glover paired up with Patrick, and the ill-assorted group gradually meandered to the front doors and the carriages.

With six in the party, two carriages had to be taken. Geoff sent Patrick to sit with Lady Rushton and young Emma in the Glover's closed carriage. He took up Eleanor and her older sister, Miss Glover, in his town coach.

After handing Miss Glover up the steps, he turned to offer his assistance to Eleanor. She took his hand, and then hesitated. Looking up into his face, she said, "It is very good of you to give up your pleasure for us."

"Oh, this is my pleasure," he corrected, the polite nothing slipping out in an automatic response. It was the sort of nonsense one spouted to ladies. He had learned that much over the past few months in London.

She eyed him, her expression serious, then shook her head. "I doubt you shall believe that in another hour."

And then she stepped up into the carriage, leaving him frowning at her and irritated. Devil take her! Either she said nothing, or her words came out too blunt. And what did she think him, anyway? An oaf with no polish? He had been shopping with ladies before—some of them respectable, most of them not. He knew how to admire their selections, praise their taste, and weave some pleasant flirtation into the process.

But she acted as if they were all headed for imprisonment in the Tower.

Devil take it, but it could not be all that bad to squire four women about a few shops for a few hours. And he vowed to himself to make it so.

The rain held off as they toured Mr. Wedgwood's showrooms in York Street, St. James's Square. But Lady Rushton had obviously given firm instructions to her daughters on their behavior. All of them, even the saucy-eyed Emma, acted like automatons of virtue. They spoke only when spoken to. They kept their observations to worries over the worsening weather, which had now added a cold bite to the December wind. And in all matters, they deferred to his taste.

If he admired a vase in Wedgwood blue, Eleanor found it lovely. If he looked at a set of teacups, Lady Rushton said at once that Eleanor must have them, and Eleanor dutifully agreed. Some demon tempted him to admire something vastly hideous, but he held back, for these choices he knew would end up shortly enough at Westerley and he dared not risk it.

With the sky darkening, they went on to Charles Blyde,

cabinet-maker and upholster. And Geoff thought with an inner sigh that it really was too bad that it was not flooding, so that he would have an excellent excuse to end this day.

But he was, he vowed to himself, enjoying it.

At Blyde's, Eleanor ordered a writing desk. Or, that is, Geoff watched as her mother ferreted out his tastes and then chose something for her daughter.

He began to worry that his bride had no will or thoughts of her own. And he could not help but compare her to Cynthia.

Cynthia would have found a way to tease him out of his dark mood. She would have made fun of his taste, and would have chosen for herself with that impeccable sense of style he had seen in her since her family had first moved to the village at Westerley. What had she been? Eleven? No, twelve. That was right. He had been sixteen and just about to go off to Oxford, and he'd been heart-struck at once by her wheat-golden hair and her bright silver-gray eyes and sprite-like figure. She had grown up during the years, but she had never lost that sense of girlish, fey charm.

"What do you think? Will this rain hold off for one more hour?"

Geoffrey glanced around to realize that they now stood outside Mr. Blyde's shop and that Patrick had addressed him.

He blushed at his own poor manners in drifting off to another world—a world both past and a future forever lost. It had been his own fault that he had lost it. And now, here he was punishing Lady Rushton and her daughters with his lack of attention.

Forcing a smile, he decided he would make amends to them. He glanced up, measuring the sky. The darkening clouds had not yet deepened to the black that boded a soaking rain. "I think we might at least manage a stop at

Schomberg House for refreshments. Some tea or chocolate?"

Patrick stared at him, surprise rising on his face, but Emma's expression at once lit up and even the quiet Elizabeth said, "Oh, yes. Please, Mother, may we?"

Lady Rushton hesitated, then said, "Well, I suppose it would indeed be a nice treat."

Eleanor said nothing, Geoffrey noticed. But no one else seemed to pay any heed to that.

It was but a few minutes drive to Schomberg House, a handsome, four-storey mansion, built for the Duke of Schomberg in the late sixteen hundreds, but now converted into shops that offered small furniture, drapery hangings, and refreshments to those worn out by their efforts in spending money.

Eleanor looked about her, hanging back a little from the others as they entered and mounted the staircase. She had not visited here before, but she knew from reading her London guidebooks that Thomas Gainsborough had lived and painted here until 1788. That such a famous artist had occupied the house awed Eleanor, and she stared about her, wondering what he had found to inspire him to greatness.

A deep voice pulled her out of her thoughts. "Miss Eleanor?"

She glanced up into Lord Staines's handsome face. Expecting to see a frown, relief eased into her when she saw that a smile softened his mouth instead.

He gestured to the baroque grandeur, the gilt and carved wood. "Are you lost in admiration?"

"Actually, I was wondering if grand rooms inspire grand thoughts. Or do they too often instead inspire grand ambitions, and grand arrogance?"

He cocked his head and his eyes took on a sparkle. "I was about to say we have even more impressive stairs at

Westerley, but now I fear I would be inviting comparison to arrogance or ambition."

Her face heated. "I did not mean . . . that is, I should have known you would have at least one house this grand."

Still smiling, he seemed not at all inclined to take her words amiss. "I have many more, and I can assure you that the ambition they tend to inspire is to keep them all well-roofed and managed. And the arrogance is tempered by the rest of the world's inability to conform with one's wishes."

Stopping at the top of the stairs, she regarded him. He had spoken with a light and teasing tone, but there was that look in his eyes again. That deeply wounded and defensive look. What was it that he had wished for that had not come to him?

He glanced at her, puzzled, that wounded look vanishing from his eyes. Then he offered his arm to lead her into the room on the second floor where the proprietors served tea, sweetmeats, wine, and coffee.

"Come," he said, "Let me find you a seat near the windows. There is a fine view of St. James's Park, and out to the Surrey Hills as well, but I doubt we'll see so far today, given the weather."

A little shy of him, she put her hand on his arm. He led her forward, talking about the quality of the refreshments to be had and offering stories about the room, which had once served as the breakfast room of the house. He seemed to be going out of his way to be pleasant, and she began to relax a little.

At the table, Emma was chattering, talking about all they had seen and bought, and she quizzed Elizabeth and Lord Staines's brother on what had been the best bargain of the day. And Lady Rushton soon engaged Lord Staines in a discussion of the upcoming wedding and the invitations to be sent.

Eleanor had nothing to add to any of this. She smiled as Lord Staines ordered her tea. And then she sat there and stared out the window at the dampening street.

Once, Emma asked about the tea set Eleanor had bought, if she did not indeed prefer the other pattern of strawberry leaves. Unable to even remember what had been picked out, Eleanor merely smiled, said she was content, and went back to staring out the window.

Fat rain drops had started to fall against the panes and onto the street below. The park lay empty, its trees already barren of leaves. And just down the way, Eleanor glimpsed a donkey-cart being loaded.

She could just make out the forlorn figure of the gray donkey, its ears flattened back and its head low. As she watched, the goods piled higher and higher in the cart behind the small donkey.

The poor thing will never pull all that, she thought, anxiety tightening inside her as if someone had asked her to carry that load herself.

Just then, the cart's owner came forward, a ragged, thin man with a black, wide-brimmed hat pulled low against the wet. He tugged on the donkey's reins. The donkey strained forward in its harness, and then stopped. And the man's arm rose and fell, and Eleanor flinched as if she had heard the whip crack next to her.

She looked away from the window.

Lord Staines had that bored look on his face, but her mother held his full attention with details of guests to be invited for the wedding—which was set for Christmas Eve—and how to keep the list reasonable. Lord Staines's brother—Mr. Westerley—held both Emma and Elizabeth spellbound with stories about the recent political upheavals, which included the facts behind Lord Castlereagh's duel with George Canning, and tales of the late Duke of Portland, the former Prime Minister, falling asleep as he read over state papers with his Cabinet.

Eleanor's stare wandered back to the scene outside the window. She did not care about duels and Prime Ministers—alive or dead. But she did care for those poor creatures who suffered in silence, and who could not defend themselves.

The donkey was still there, struggling with its impossible load.

Forcing her gaze away, she told herself that she could not help. Besides, it would be rude to leave. And it was really none of her business.

She sat staring into her half-empty tea cup, but she could not still the tears of her heart.

Very quietly she said, "Pardon me a moment." No one seemed to notice as she rose and stole out from the room.

What she missed seeing as she fled, however, was Lord Staines glancing up, noticing her empty chair and starting to look for her.

Four

Geoff had known his bride to make herself invisible before, but never before quite so literally. *Where the devil had she gotten to?* Irritated that he had not noticed her departure, he wondered if she had left to find a convenience. Well, she would return. Bored, and wishing he were not, his gaze moved to the window.

It had started to rain. They would all be damp by the time they reached home. Ah, well, it could not be helped.

And then he sat up.

There on the street below he glimpsed a small fawn-clad figure striding across the lane, her step purposeful.

The devil take her, what was she doing out there?

Rising, he interrupted Lady Rushton's plans for including second cousins and those more distant connections on the guest list for the breakfast after the wedding. "My dear lady, I shall leave that to you, and to my father's discretion. Westerley is still his house, after all. Now, you must excuse me a moment. Patrick, see if you can find the ladies' wraps, and perhaps they would like a tour of the shops before we go. I'll have the coaches brought 'round, and come find you."

Before anyone could argue with him, or do more than stare at him, he turned and strode for the door, his temper simmering, and too aware of Patrick's worried stare on his back. His brother had a right to his misgivings. Geoff wished for nothing so much right now as to sit Miss Eleanor down and blister her ears with a lecture on how future countesses were supposed to behave. And it was not with them waltzing along London streets by themselves.

Outside Schomberg House, the heavy sky now drizzled a hesitant rain. It did nothing to dampen Geoff's irritation, but it did make him realize that he had stepped out without his hat. A fine sight he must look. The pulse throbbed in his tightened jaw. That was her fault, as well, for putting him into such an unreasonable hurry.

He glanced around and saw that the porter beside the door had already unfurled a black umbrella and raised it over them. The man, stiff-faced and dressed in a red livery said nothing as Geoff pulled out a guinea and pressed it into the man's gloved hand.

"For the umbrella," Geoff said. A moment later, he started down the steps, umbrella in hand.

A coach and pair rushed past, making him stop. Then he strode across the unpaved road, the sodden ground squelching under his step and the wet manure starting to stink. Once he had crossed, Geoff's stare narrowed as he sought his quarry. The rain made it difficult to see, and he had not the advantage now of the view that he'd had from the room upstairs.

Then he caught a glimpse of movement, and he started forward, brushing past a woman in black who hurried to shelter, her head down and her black bonnet limp with rain.

And that's what my bride-to-be ought to be doing, Geoff thought, his temper simmering even hotter until it more than covered his fear for her being alone on any London byway.

Then he realized that Eleanor was no longer headed away from him. She seemed to have stopped beside a donkey cart, and now stood there, stroking the donkey's wet face, talking to the cart driver as if pleasantly passing the time.

His step faltered.

What the devil was she doing?

The cart driver towered over Eleanor, ragged and wretched looking, but also smiling foolishly, his hat off and held in his hands, his thinning, dark hair slicked to his head. A second fellow stood nearby with his arms folded, his hat pulled low and a sullen look on his pinched face. He kept pulling out a gold watch, glancing at it, and tucking it away again.

With a smile, Eleanor left off petting the donkey to fumble in the small reticule that hung on her arm. To the cart driver's grinning delight, she pulled out a slim leather purse and handed over some coins. There was an interchange of words between the driver and the other man, who then moved forward to reluctantly drag a chair from the cart.

Geoff stared at the scene, baffled. He tried to summon back his anger for Eleanor having placed herself in danger. But the only peril that seemed to loom over her at the moment was a soaking from the rain—and his own rapidly cooling temper. He felt almost foolish now as he stood there, wondering what he should do. He started forward again, at least determined to reclaim his fiancée.

". . . most intelligent donkey," Eleanor was saying. "Now be certain you bring him to this address when you have done with Mr. Appleby's furniture."

"Oh, yes, miss. But of course, miss."

"And I trust that with the season of good will upon us, Mr. Appleby, you will not try to short Mr. Ferguson again by making any more of his donkeys carry a double load for the price of one."

Appleby scowled. "He said the beast could . . ."

"I said he could take a full cart," Ferguson interrupted.

"And that's what it is," Appleby shot back.

Geoff tensed to step between the two men, who now glared at each other, nostrils distended and chests punched forward like fighting roosters. Eleanor was there before him.

"Gentleman, this point is moot. Mr. Ferguson has already accepted my offer, so the donkey is mine and I will dictate his load. And, further, Mr. Appleby, I will remind you that the Good Book tells us that Mary herself rode a donkey to Bethlehem. It is a most noble animal, and ought to be treated with due respect."

His face reddening, Mr. Appleby grumbled, but he ducked his head, finally muttered a reluctant apology and then turned back to easing the cart's load.

With her heart light, Eleanor turned to hurry back to the others. Instead, she nearly collided with Lord Staines.

He stood there, hatless, an umbrella slanting over his shoulder, and a soft nimbus of dampness clinging to his golden hair. He was frowning, and he looked as magnificent and daunting as had that staircase in Schomberg House.

Fumbling with the stings to her reticule, she said the only thing that came to mind. "Oh, hullo."

His expression hardened, and those blue eyes flashed like lightning in a clear sky. "Hullo, indeed. So you have found something at last that you truly wished to buy—a donkey."

"It is a rather fine donkey," she stammered, her fingers cold and knotting the strings of her reticule and all too aware that her donkey wasn't the least bit a fine anything. She became aware now of her damp shoulders, of the bedraggled feather on her bonnet that clung to her cheek. She must look a fright. But a touch of irritation flared as well.

Why did he have to follow her? Why must he put

himself into this when she would much rather that he not do so!

Lord Staines glanced at the poor donkey, whose damp, gray hair now stood in rain-soaked spikes. The animal had begun to give off the ripe, earthy odor of wet donkey.

"And what plans do you have for such a fine beast?" he asked, stressing the fine with a heavy sarcasm.

Taking the high road, she said, "I thought I would send him home."

His frown darkened. "To Westerley?"

She winced and twisted her reticule's strings even tighter. She had been thinking of Rushton Manor as her home—and the donkey's. She had not remembered that she would not return to her father's country estate unless it was as a guest.

Anxiety rose in her. Would he forbid her to keep her donkey? It would be within his rights, for when she married all that she had became his. Chin down, she stared up at him, uncertain what to say or do, wishing he would stop looking so forbidding. It was just too unfair that he did not look as bedraggled in the rain as she felt.

Geoff shifted the umbrella to his other hand and arranged it so that it covered more of Eleanor than it did of him. With a pair of enormous brown eyes turned up on him, he found himself unable to voice the lecture that he ought to give. She had been foolish and heedless, but he did not have the heart to put any more apprehension into those eyes.

Suppressing the urge to reach out his hand and flick that bedraggled brown ostrich feather from her pale cheek, he glanced at the sorry beast she had bought—for too much money, no doubt.

"Have him sent to Westerley then. We shall just have to find some place in the stables for him."

Her face brightened. "Oh, thank you."

In an instant, she caught him in an impulsive hug, her

arms wrapping around him with surprising strength, nearly knocking the umbrella from his grip. Small, firm breasts pressed against his chest. Her warmth mingled with his. Her bonnet scraped his cheek. The smell of wet donkey and orange blossom wove around him.

And his pulse shot up like a fireworks rocket at the Vauxhall pleasure gardens.

She seemed to recall the proprieties at once, for she stepped away, the color charming and rosy on her cheeks, her eyes large and seeming more black than brown. A flash of something else flickered in her eyes, an instant's intriguing glimmer, and then she looked down to fuss with her purse and brush at her cheek and present him a view of the top of her sodden bonnet.

His own reaction shamed him. The urge to pull her back into his arms stirred inside him, and the image of kissing her, here on the misting street with only this umbrella to shelter their faces from the road, flashed sweet and hot. He banished those thoughts with an inward curse at his own low instincts. He had learned some control with his practice of sin during the past season.

But still his pulse beat fast, even as he tried to at least act like a gentleman.

"We shall be late," he said, his words short. He took her arm with his hand, even though he knew that he should offer his arm and allow her to lay her hand lightly upon it. Damn the protocols. And damn the niceties. He had learned nine months ago that he was no gentleman. At this moment, this was about as close he could come to being one.

He hurried her forward. Her skirt brushed against his legs, and she had to take two steps for every one of his.

Just before crossing the street, he paused and glanced down at her.

For a giddy instant Eleanor thought that he meant to swing her up in his arms and carry her across. But he merely looked away, a tight set to his beautiful mouth and the lightning back in his eyes, and then he hurried her across the mud to Schomberg House. He must be very angry.

She struggled to keep up with him, wishing that she had the courage to complain. But she didn't trust her voice. Not with his hand tight on her arm, and with her heart pounding so fast. Only it was not his hurrying her that left her feeling light-headed and short of breath. She was such a little idiot to react to something as simple as his hand on her arm.

Besides, she deserved whatever punishment he gave her. Her face burned as she thought of how she had hugged him. Hugged! In the road. With others looking on. No wonder he had stiffened. And no wonder his eyes flashed and looked darker than the skies overhead. She had acted like a child.

He returned her to the others without saying anything. No one else said anything, either, about Eleanor's sodden state. However, she caught the sideways glance from her mother, and she knew there would be questions later. She did not really care, however. Her mind was fully caught up in wondering if Lord Staines would now find her actions horrible enough to cry off from marrying her.

Four days later Eleanor still had not heard anything to indicate that Lord Staines had changed his mind. Her mother had lectured her, when they got home that wet day, on having ruined her gown. It did not help matters that Schomberg—for that was what Eleanor had decided to call the donkey—had arrived later that afternoon, and she had had to explain his presence, and the circumstances of his acquisition.

At the end of the story, Eleanor's mother had sighed, shook her head and muttered darkly, "When you are married, things will be different."

Eleanor had almost asked how they would be different, but a glance at her mother's exasperated expression made her change her mind and meekly offer to start writing out wedding invitations.

That task soon had bored Eleanor into staring out the window, watching the raindrops fall. And she kept thinking instead how it had felt to press herself against Lord Staines, and how he had taken her arm and had swept her away. She let out a deep sigh. He had swept her away because he had been cross with her, not because he wanted to sweep her anywhere.

Would she spend her entire life with him making him cross?

It seemed a strong possibility.

A short two days later, Lord Rushton had announced they would be setting off for Westerley on the morrow. Lady Rushton protested that they had not bought everything needed, and he answered with a smile that she would have to be satisfied with buying out the shops in Guildford, the nearest market town to Westerley.

The news had put everyone in a bustle, but there was still time enough for one last event. The engagement ball.

Eleanor had been dreading it. She would have to smile until her face ached. Even worse, she would have to endure everyone watching her and talking about her. And when it came time to dress for dinner, it took the efforts of all of her sisters to get her into her gown and keep her from bolting from the house.

"I think I am going to be ill," Eleanor said, her stomach churning and a leaden weight in her chest.

"Nonsense. You are simply worrying too much," Elizabeth said, as she coaxed Eleanor's hair into ringlets with the curling tongs. She patted a curl into place, and then put the iron tongs back to heat again by the fire so that she could curl the next strand.

"But to have all those people staring at me . . ."

Eleanor broke off, unable even to bear the thought of being the center of so much attention.

Emma gave up admiring her own white gown trimmed with cream ribbons and came over to give her sister's shoulders a squeeze. "Well, stop thinking of it if it so upsets you. Mama never allows unpleasant thoughts to upset her, so why should you?"

Eleanor glanced at Emma's cheerful reflection in the mirror on the dressing table. "What should I think of instead?"

"Why not think of Lord Staines?" Emma dimpled, and her eyes sparkled with mischief. "If I were engaged to him, he certainly would occupy my thoughts, as well as all my other senses."

"Emma, really!" Elizabeth scolded, frowning at her sister.

"Well, he would," Emma insisted.

Eleanor let out a sigh. He had been occupying all too much of her mind. He had not been pleased with her at Schomberg House, but she so wished she could please him tonight. That was the only thing keeping her from complaining of illness and keeping to her bed. And so she had wanted to look radiant. Lovely. Breathaking.

"I look like a ghost," she muttered, staring at her pale reflection and her white gown.

After wrapping another lock of wavy brown hair into the curling tongs, Elizabeth glanced down at Eleanor. "You look charming. And a touch of pallor is suitable in a bride-to-be."

"She does look like a ghost," Evelyn said from her seat on Eleanor's bed. "And I smell burning hair."

Elizabeth let out a cry and pulled the tongs out of Eleanor's hair, but the curl was only crimped too tight and not terribly singed. Shoulders slumping, Eleanor watched her sisters fuss with combs and flowers to hide the now too-curly strands.

Now I look like a ghost with too-curly hair. But she would not say that, for it would only hurt her sisters' feelings, and they were working so hard to try and make her look pretty.

Satisfied at last, Elizabeth left to allow Eleanor's maid to help Eleanor finish dressing. Emma and Evelyn left as well, but Emma came back with a pot of rouge, and whispered, "Mama won't notice just a touch."

Eleanor allowed Emma to smudge the rouge on, but when Emma had gone, Eleanor rubbed her skin fiercely. She couldn't bring herself to paint her face, something their mother scorned for any lady. Besides, it seemed too much like inviting even more notice of herself. Then she took a deep breath, took another one, took a third, and finally found the courage to leave her room.

At the top of the stairs, Eleanor paused to drop a kiss on Evelyn's head. Too young to come downstairs, Evelyn had positioned herself where she could watch the guests arrive. Now, she frowned, her forehead scrunching with lines. "Perhaps you ought to use your card to ask for a green velvet dress. You would look very well in green, you know."

A smile welled up inside her and Eleanor bent down to hug her sister. "Should I ask instead if you can come to live with us?"

"Oh, yes, do. But not all the time. I should miss mama and papa too much. Will you miss them, Ellie? And us?"

For an instant tears stung the back of Eleanor's eyes. She forced a bright smile and hugged Evelyn even tighter. "I shall not. For I shall see you too often to miss you. And now, what do you want me to spirit away from the ball for you?"

"Champagne. Just one glass, please?"

Eleanor knew that she ought not to promise such indulgence, but she could not resist her sister's pleading eyes. And so she promised, and then she went downstairs. Two hours later, she wished she could sneak away to keep her promise to Evelyn. But Lord Staines had still not arrived, and guests were starting to talk about his absence.

Only the family and close relations had been at dinner. Lord Staines and his brothers had sent their regrets that they could not attend dinner, but Lord Staines's note had said he would be at the ball.

But where was he?

He had not come by eleven, when her parents had reluctantly moved away from the receiving line beside the ballroom doors. Had something happened to him? Or was this perhaps his way of giving her a reason to break the engagement?

That notion had her stomach tightening even worse than it had in anticipation of this ball.

Glancing around the crowded ballroom with a smile locked in place, Eleanor whispered to Elizabeth, "I think my face is going to be stuck like this forever."

"Perhaps if you smile long enough you will actually start enjoying yourself."

Eleanor forced her smile wider as Lady Terrance and her daughter came to wish her happy and ask how soon Lord Staines would be arriving. Eleanor froze, but Elizabeth made up vague excuses that seemed to satisfy the ladies.

As Lady Terrance moved away, Eleanor cast another worried glance toward the entrance. "He is not going to come, is he?"

"Of course he will. He has to," Elizabeth insisted, her bright tone sounding forced.

Eleanor opened her mouth to object to this lack of logic, but before she could say anything, a stir brushed through the room. She glanced at the entrance to the ballroom—heads were turning in that direction. And when the crowd parted slightly, there stood Lord Staines.

Five

Eleanor looked very young, Geoff decided at once. Very young, very innocent in white, and better than he deserved. A slash of rosy hue stood out on her cheeks, making those brown eyes of hers enormous, and her simple, high-waisted gown showed her trim figure to advantage. Well, why should she not shine tonight? This was her night to celebrate that she was to marry an earl's heir. A great catch in anyone's book, except perhaps in his own. And Cynthia's.

Scowling, he glanced around the ballroom, decorated in garlands of pine with white candles. He had delayed too long his arrival, he knew. It had been badly done. But it had taken the better part of a bottle of brandy just to get him here, and to push aside the unwelcome memories raised by that damn letter.

Blindly, he turned, found a drink offered on a silver tray. He took it, drained it, put the glass back, and took a second. He hardly knew what he was drinking, or with whom he had just smiled at or shaken hands. He went through the motions, but in his mind, he kept seeing Cynthia's heartbreakingly lovely face.

This should have been our engagement ball.

Someone else said something to him, and he nodded,

smiled and turned away, his loathing for himself growing at his bad manners. He could not seem to help himself.

Damn, but why did that letter have to come this afternoon, of all times? He could not curse Mrs. Fletcher, Cynthia's mother, for writing him news of the neighborhood, and with warm wishes for his nuptials. Ah, if only that had been all there was to it. But, no, Mrs. Fletcher's regret that he and Cynthia had not made a match of it had stained every line, every sentiment.

And her regrets had returned to him everything that he had spent the last nine months striving to forget.

He had cried off dinner with Eleanor's family because he knew he would be poor company. *Poor*. He would have been bloody awful. With Patrick and Andrew already gone ahead to Westerley, he did not have them to act as buffers between him and the Glovers. And he did not have them acting as his conscience to behave himself.

No, he had only his memories of Cynthia.

Exchanging his empty glass for a full one, he drank that as well. Why could he not at least get drunk? Why did his mind seem sharper with each glass? His sins as clear as the crystal goblet in his hand?

Someone else took his hand to shake and wished him happy, and he somehow found a smile that he could stiffen onto his face. Then he knew that he had better search out his bride and her father and get this over with before he ruined everything. He was far too good at that.

And so he put aside his empty glass, took up a full one, and tried to remember that he was a gentleman, and that he had a duty to his wife-to-be tonight.

Watching Lord Staines make his way towards her, Eleanor thought he looked the ideal of masculine perfection. From his golden locks brushed into careless curls, to his black coat that set off his wide shoulders, to his white knee-breeches, white stockings, and black dancing slippers. Perfect, except for the steady supply of drink in his hand.

Biting her lower lip, she watched him, her senses alert and every instinct inside her clamoring that something was wrong. Something dark and dangerous shimmered at the back of his too-bright eyes. She did not know what she might do to smooth it away, and she feared that perhaps some unhappiness with her had put it there.

He came up to her, and she lowered her gaze, afraid she would be tempted into asking him what was wrong, and that was hardly a way for a lady to greet her affianced husband.

Then she heard Elizabeth say, her voice deliberate and cool, "Lord Staines, how nice that you could join us at last. I vow that some here thought you had changed your plans—to attend, that is."

Eleanor shot an astonished glance at her sister. Elizabeth was never so rude as to offer such deliberate undertones of disapproval.

In fact, Elizabeth looked rather like the ideal match to Lord Staines. Candlelight pulled gold glints from her brown hair. She was nearly the same height, and held her head high to look straight at him. The pearls quivering around her slim throat were the only betrayal that she was not as confident in challenging him as she seemed.

Elizabeth held Lord Staines's gaze with a hard stare, and a rush of affection swept through Eleanor that Lizzy should leap to her defense. Then she glanced at Lord Staines, a little afraid for her sister.

He returned Elizabeth's stare with one just as direct, and then he turned to Eleanor. "Is that what you thought? That I would not come?"

Eleanor curled her toes inside her silk slippers. She did not want to tell him that she had indeed believed him capable of such behavior. He did not look as if he needed any more lashings added to his soul tonight. Instead, she wet her lips, and said, "I had understood that you do not care what others think of you, so I am not certain why you should ask me that."

The corner of his mouth crooked. "We are speaking of you, not others. Now, pray excuse us, Miss Glover. I should like to take a stroll around the room with your sister."

He offered his arm to Eleanor, and she could only give Elizabeth what was meant to be a reassuring glance before setting her hand on that muscular arm.

As they set off, the crowd parted for them. Eleanor kept her lashes lowered, watching her hem swirl around her feet and brush his ankles.

Beside her, Lord Staines said, his voice hesitant, "I am sorry if I put you in an awkward position this evening."

His too-careful speech told her that he had indeed drunk a good deal tonight. Her heart ached for him. What was wrong?

"Please don't apologize. You put me in an awkward position when you proposed. I mean, that is, I expected the engagement to be aw—" Biting off the word, she glanced up at him.

A faint amusement warmed his tired eyes. "Awkward? Awful? Or is there another adjective that I am missing?"

She shook her head and would say nothing more.

He nodded to others as they passed, but he did not pause to allow them to interrupt. Then he said, his voice low, enticing her confidence, "You might as well tell me. You cannot make it any worse."

"Yes, I can." She felt his stare on her, burning into her head, but she would not meet it. "Father says that I have a tongue as blunt as a dull garden spade."

She heard his chuckle and she did glance up then. His face had relaxed, and under her hand the tension eased from his arm. A thread of pleasure spiraled loose inside her, like a kite set free on the wind. She had made him laugh. She could make him smile. She felt as if he had just given her a wonderful gift.

"Well, please do not sharpen it. I like you blunt, Eleanor."

She smiled and ducked her chin low, holding close the delight that his words had raised in her, and then she looked up at him again. "Even so, you almost did not come tonight."

He stopped and something dark shadowed his smile. "Engagements are like a game of Cricket—almosts do not count. And I am here now. And I have a Christian name, which I now give you free right to use."

Geoffrey, she said inside her mind, turning the word over, liking the sound of it, but too shy to say it aloud, for in saying his name she might say to him far too much of other things she did not want revealed.

Turning, he signaled a waiter and got them glasses of wine. He gave her one and took the other. "Shall we find our courage in the glass, and then let us find your father and get this announcement over with?" He hesitated suddenly, his blue eyes pale. "Unless, that is . . . I do not want to rob you of this moment. If this is something you have dreamed of . . ."

She had, in a fashion, but her fancies had not been anything like this, so she said without a second thought, "Oh, I never would have spent my blank card on this."

His smile widened, and he lifted his glass. "Then let us drink to getting over this hurdle as best we may."

With a shy smile, she lifted her glass to ring the crystal against his. Then she frowned and asked, "But I would make one request of you, if I may?"

"A request—but not written on a card? Does it have to do with donkeys?" he asked, a teasing spark back in his eyes.

She started turning the glass in her hand, twisting the stem between her fingers. "No, no animals. And no card—unless you feel I ought to. It is just that . . . Well, that is . . . how do you do that . . . that whatever-you-did when you came into the room? How do you look as if you do not care? I wish I could look so . . . so unconcerned and confident. Can you teach that to me?"

His smile slanted, and the look in his eyes deadened to something that sent a chill across Eleanor's skin. "That is not something I ever want to teach you. And I pray that life may spare you the lesson I was given on how not to care so much. Now, come. Your father is looking as impatient as I feel."

Taking her arm, he led her towards Lord Rushton, and the announcement to be made.

Eleanor wondered if it was how she had asked her question, or if something else was behind his curt response. She wished suddenly that she knew more of the man who would be her husband.

I can always cry off. If it really gets too awful, father and mother would let me do so, she told herself. But she feared she would never be brave or wise enough ever to do so.

And then her father was signaling the musicians to stop playing, and everyone was turning to look at her, and the old panic tightened inside her chest like a frightened, wild animal that was about to burst out of her.

She tried to keep breathing. She tried to remember Emma's smiles and Elizabeth's advice. She tried not to notice all the stares focused on her, or the ladies whispering behind their fans, or the gentlemen with knowing looks on their faces.

They are laughing at me because I am no match for him, she knew, and she wanted to shrink herself into nothing.

It doesn't matter. I don't care what they think.

But it did. And she did.

They all kept staring at her, watching. And she could not bear it a second longer. She had to get away.

Six

Eleanor's hand tugged on Geoff's arm and he half turned towards her, expecting that she wanted something. Then he saw her face. Bewilderment, irritation, and the fear that it was happening again mixed inside him in a swirling confusion.

Devil take it, but she looked ready to bolt.

Not again, he thought, clamping his arm to his side to trap her hand against him and prevent her flight. It had been bad enough when Cynthia had fled, and that had only been during a small affair at Westerley. His pride could not endure another woman running from him, and certainly not in the midst of a London ball.

And then he realized that she was not looking at him. Her fear seemed to be focused on the crowd around them.

At least it's not me, he thought. Relief coursed through him, easing the tension in his back. Still, it would not do to have her run from his side as if he were a monster, or she a fool. He glanced around, seeking the source of her distress, but saw nothing out of the ordinary. He looked back down at her.

Fear lay stark in a pale sheen on her skin. Her chest rose and fell with rapid, shallow breaths, and her eyes had lightened to the color of weak tea. What the devil had frightened her?

The crowd closed around them, glances speculative as Lord Rushton asked those assembled to take up a glass and toast the happy couple, and then he beamed and the crowd pressed closer to offer their best wishes. Eleanor muttered something, and tried to tug her arm free. Geoff realized then what it must be.

Of course. The crowd. The attention. She had asked him if he could teach her how to look uncaring. And had his future countess not perfected her art of disappearing to avoid just such situations as these?

A touch of displeasure tugged a frown from him. How the devil could she act a countess if she could not even bear this small amount of attention?

He glanced down at that pale face, thinking that his annoyance would deepen, but instead his mood softened.

She looked like a fawn caught by a pack of slavering hounds. She had stopped tugging on his arm, and seemed to be trying her best to withstand the stares, but he could see that she winced at each whispered speculation as if under a lash. Her stare remained fixed on the floor, and he could readily believe she was trying to will the parquet to part and swallow her.

The tightness around his mouth and his chest loosened.

She had asked for his help, and that should count for something. It also meant that he ought to do something. Only he would need both hands free if he were to do anything.

Glancing around, he found one of the other Glover girls—Emma, he thought it was—on his other side. He thrust his empty wine glass at her, and she took it, her response automatic and her eyebrows rising in surprise. But he only turned and took Eleanor's glass from her hand and thrust it at Emma as well. Let her juggle the dashed crystal.

Eleanor glanced up at him, her eyes glazed and distant. Before she could do more, he captured her hand firmly in his and then tucked his arm around her waist, quite aware that even though they were engaged he was taking shocking liberties to so hold her. Society, however, would expect no less of a gentleman with his reputation, and Eleanor hardly seemed to notice.

"Look at me," he ordered, his voice low and firm.

She glanced up, and her throat moved with a convulsive swallow. "Please. I don't feel well. You must excuse me."

"And you will have to forgive me later, for I'm not letting you go anywhere. No, don't look at them," he commanded, as her frightened stare fixed on the crowd again. "Look at me. Only me. I am the only one who matters here. Not them. Not their chatter."

A brief smile barely lifted her lips and then disappeared. "You must think me the worst coward."

"I think that if you really wish to learn how to act like an arrogant, smug dolt, such as myself, then you must focus upon me to learn my secrets."

The lines eased from her tightened forehead, and he wished that they were in private so that he could drop a grateful kiss upon that now smooth brow. But if he kissed his intended in front of everyone and God that *would* cause a sensation. Lord, but it tempted him to do so. Only she'd bolt for certain then.

He glanced at the avid stares cast at him—and Eleanor—at the speculation in the ladies' eyes; at the commiserating looks from the gentlemen who knew that they, too, must someday marry to please their families, not themselves. And a desire—clear and certain—rose in him to shield this wretched, trembling girl next to him from all these damnable gossips.

"The first trick," he said, leaning down to whisper into her ear, "is to imagine they are all naked."

She pulled back, alarmed, her cheeks as pink as a child's. "Naked?"

He glanced around him, noticed that others had heard her. Lovely, he had just made things even worse.

"Well, not completely so, but in their shifts with their garters and stockings showing, and their faces red from the shame of it."

She lifted her stare just for a moment to scan the room, and her lips twitched slightly before she lost her courage again and her glance dropped. Well, it was progress.

"And now," he went on, keeping his tone light, trying to put into it every ounce of coaxing charm that he owned, "I want you to tell me if you care what I think of you?"

Her stare flew up to his face, and her lips parted and trembled. For an instant, he was struck with the desperate need in her eyes. He knew that feeling too well. She glanced away. When she looked back, she had mastery of herself again and had hidden away whatever desires had seemed about to be revealed.

"I want to please you," she said. "I am to be your wife."

Voice harsh, he told her, "Well, stop caring. Think of pleasing yourself."

"If I were to do that, I would leave," she muttered, a stubborn threat of rebellion rising in her voice.

There might be hope for her, he thought, a smile loosening inside him. "And so you shall," he said. "So think of an exit to make. Do you want a sweeping one?"

"A quick one. I want to be unnoticed."

"Then do not notice others. You know that trick. I've seen you use it."

Her glance rose up to his, startled, but the glazed, mindless panic in her eyes had receded. At least he had distracted her.

"What do you mean? I don't have any tricks."

"Yes, you do. A dozen at least. Tricks that let you vanish as if you're made of mist. You can't make yourself disappear just now, but you can make others disappear from your notice if you but turn that trick around. What do you think about when you want to become invisible?"

She wet her lips and hesitated, and he wondered if she would be honest with him. But then she said, her voice firm, "I just pretend I am part of the chair, or that I really am a flower on the wall coverings."

"Good. Then just picture everyone here as furniture. That fellow over there with the large stomach, he ought to be an over-stuffed divan. And the too-tall, too-thin lady surely is a standing candelabra."

Covering her mouth, Eleanor stifled a smile. "You really should not say so."

"If it amuses you, I would say anything," he said, and then he smiled down at her, his blue eyes glinting and warm, the smallest dimple appearing at the left corner of his mouth.

Eleanor's heart skipped to a faster beat, and this time not from fear. She stared up at him, fascinated by the silver glints in his blue eyes and the endless depths that seemed to draw her towards them. Awareness of the others in the room—the cloying perfumes, the hum of whispers, the drone of her father's speech about the alliance of these two families—still hovered near, just as did her fear, but it no longer swamped her. She no longer felt as if an ocean wave were about to close over her head.

The fear that had haunted her since childhood lay close, drumming under her skin with a hot urgency. She no longer worried that all the whispers must be condemning her. But she dared not lose the warmth of his arm around her waist, and the sight of his blue eyes smiling down at her.

Gratitude that he stood between her and them made her glance shyly up to him. "Thank you," she said, and meant it deeply.

His smile twisted with a cynical touch. "It is not something to thank me for, that I shall give you hard armor.

But if you so desire, I shall toughen you so that you can walk with kings, and even make you able to speak before Parliament."

For a moment, the image flashed in her mind of herself as daring and bold as he. Scornful, sweeping in and out of ballrooms. Proud and haughty. She twisted her mouth to one side. She'd be more like to trip on her hem if walking with any king, and she would be tongue-tied with terror if she even had to stand before Parliament to give them a good-day.

"I would settle for simply not shaking like a blancmange pudding set on a trotting horse every time someone looks at me."

He gave her a grin, and started to say something, but Lord Rushton had at last finished his speech and raised his glass. The toast was drunk, and then people began to press forward to shake Lord Staines's hand and wish him well, and give Eleanor sly glances that said, "And how did an insignificant girl such as you ever catch an earl's son?"

Eleanor wished that she could die.

It would be so much less painful.

Instead, she clung to Lord Staines, pressing as close as she dared to his strong, tall body. She allowed him to answer, and she pasted on a smile and muttered inaudible words to anyone who addressed her, and she tried to keep up his game of making all these strangers and acquaintances into furniture.

It helped, but nothing could ease the strain which left her temples pounding.

At last she heard Lord Staines tell those around them, "Now you must pardon us. For I have obligations elsewhere, and I would rather take leave of my intended in a more private setting."

One matron smiled coyly at him, and batted his arm with her fan, telling him he was such a rogue. And a red-faced gentlemen in a brown coat winked knowingly at him. Eleanor's face warmed, but she did not care what excuse got her from the room.

Lord Staines led her through the crowd, and she had to control her steps so that she did not seem to drag him to the doorway, even though she wanted to run ahead, pulling him with her.

When they stepped from the ballroom into the empty hall that led to the front stairs, she let out a deep breath.

Lord Staines turned an appraising stare on her. "We have run one gauntlet and survived. But I shall have to present you at court as Lady Staines after we are married, you know."

Eleanor's relief faded. "Court? Oh, no. I could not even manage my first presentation at the Queen's drawing room. That is why Emma came out this year, you know. So we could make our curtsy together. Her chatter kept me from being wretchedly ill this time on the drive to St. James's."

His expression seemed torn between a laugh and disapproval and Eleanor knew that she should not have said all that to him. But then a smile relaxed his face. "You shall have plenty of time to learn to be a countess, and I do believe I can instruct anyone in how to have an indifferent heart."

She frowned at the bitter tone that lay under his words, and almost said something, but he stopped her with a touch to her cheek. Just a light caress with the back of a bare knuckle. A soft sweep beside her mouth, and a smile that stopped her heart for an instant.

And then he gave her a short bow and turned on his heel, striding down the hall to the front entrance.

Alone in the hall, she stood quite still, listening to his firm steps on the white marble, and to the low rumble of his voice as he asked the porter at the front door for his hat and coat. Then the heavy, oak front door opened and closed, and there was nothing but the faint music from the ballroom and the fading pine scent around her from his person.

She put her hand up to her cheek, dazed, knowing that he had somehow bewitched her, and not caring that he had. He had not been disappointed in her. He had smiled at her. And he had saved her tonight.

She could have danced a jig up the stairs to her bedroom.

The click of a door latch scattered the daydreams she had started to weave. Someone else was leaving the ballroom.

Eleanor fled at once to a shadowed alcove where the half-burnt candles in the hall did not cast any light. She squeezed tight behind a statue of Diana, for she simply was not up to any more congratulations tonight.

From the ballroom, Lady Terrance and her daughter, Harriet, stepped into the hall. The sound of music and the swell of voices faded as the door closed behind them again. But Eleanor could hear their words all too clearly.

". . . sorry for the poor little thing," Lady Terrance was saying, her shrill voice quite recognizable.

"Really, mother. She is going to be a countess. What is to be sorry for there?"

"Titles do not come for free, my dear. And she will have to pay a steep price for that one. I caution you, Harriet. It is one thing to marry without love. But it is quite another to marry a gentleman who loves elsewhere. That is always disaster."

Eleanor's skin iced as their words flowed over her. *A gentleman who loves elsewhere?* She had no doubt of whom they spoke, but she had the strongest sensation that Lady Terrance's reference applied to something more than the gossip about Lord Staines's casual affairs.

A gentleman who loves elsewhere.

Lady Terrance and her daughter began to move towards

the front door, and Eleanor leaned forward, her curiosity driving her to listen, even though she knew that eavesdroppers never heard good of themselves.

"Do you think she knows?" Harriet asked, her voice eager.

"How can she not? Her mother must have cautioned her that Staines's heart had been given to another and rejected. But did I tell you what I heard Lady Davenport say about how he. . . ."

The voices faded into the shadows of the hallway, and Eleanor let them go. A hollow emptiness lay inside her, as if she were a doll whose stuffing had been pulled out.

Now she understood that wounded look that sometimes appeared in his eyes. And she understood the bitterness behind his words. He could teach anyone how to have a hard heart, because he had learned how to shield his own from everything.

No wonder he thought her a suitable choice. A sensible choice. A wife would not demand a heart already given elsewhere.

Slowly, Eleanor emerged from her hiding place, a curious numbness spreading across her skin as if she had stood for too long in the cold. Why had he not been able to marry the woman he loved? Had she died? She could not imagine any woman being unable or unwilling to return his love.

She started for the servants' stairs so that she could slip to her room unnoticed. And one thought kept repeating itself in her head. *How utterly awful to love someone and know that love cannot be returned.*

She knew exactly how awful it did feel.

By the time dawn lightened to reveal a dull sky and a depressing drizzle that slicked the pavement and streaked the windows of the Glover's townhouse with jagged slashes of wet, Eleanor had made up her mind.

She had thought it over from every angle, and she had decided that Lord Staines—Geoffrey—had been right about this from the start. She would think up something sensible to ask for, and she would settle into a comfortable marriage.

Didn't people do that all the time?

It was a marriage to an earl's heir, after all. A handsome gentleman. A kind man. Most young ladies would regard this as a Christmas wish come true. And that would be how she would view it from now on.

Today they started for Westerley. So, as of today, she would stop weaving fantasies around him. She would stop reading more into his actions than existed. She would be happy with what she had.

With that attitude fixed in her head, she dressed in a sensible dark-blue traveling dress, and while her maid laced the back she struggled with what she could ask for that would be so perfectly sensible.

Her imagination proved to be as blank as the card that lay on her dresser, as empty and barren as a snow-iced field.

Eleanor let out a deep sigh.

"Don't you like it, miss?" the maid asked, her voice high and anxious as she finished doing Eleanor's hair into a simple, upswept knot.

"Oh, no, it's fine," Eleanor said with an automatic smile and not even glancing at herself to see if it was, for it never was. Her hair inevitably fell out of whatever form it was put into, falling into straight, stray wisps at some point during the day.

Gathering up her blank card, Eleanor stuffed it into her sleeve, where it rubbed against her skin. Then she started downstairs.

Perhaps she would ask for his permission to live as she

pleased. That sounded just daring enough, and yet not too specific.

And then a thought struck her, and she paused on the carpeted stair, smiling at the utter absurdity of it, even though she knew she could never write such a thing.

But what if she did?

What if she wrote that she wanted his permission to take a lover?

She muffled a giggle behind her hand, and then slowly started downstairs, weaving the scene that would play when she presented her card. He would forget that other woman. Yes, forget her. And he would be jealous. And stormy-eyed, and it might even drive him to saying, "*So you want a lover, do you?*" And then he would sweep her into his arms and . . .

Ah, but that was not how it would go. He would probably grin, tell her that she was welcome to try, and think himself let off easily with a demand she could never achieve and for which he had to do nothing.

Shaking off the images, she started down the stairs again.

A young lady dressed in a sensible dark blue traveling dress was not the sort who ever asked for a lover. So she vowed to herself, instead, that by the time they reached Westerley she would have something to ask for.

Then they could enjoy this most joyful of seasons. Only she doubted very much if that would happen, either, for the wedding fell right in the middle of Christmas.

Perhaps I ought to ask for a late January wedding? But his father lay dying, so a delay did not seem a kind thing to request.

Stepping into the breakfast room, she greeted her parents, took her place at the table, and tried to summon an interest in any sort of food.

Around her, breakfast passed in a flurry. Evelyn kept slipping out and back into the high-ceilinged room as she remembered things she had forgotten to pack—her favorite doll, the scarf that matched her riding habit, her traveling backgammon game.

Emma was no better. She did not dash about like Evelyn, but she kept fretting that the rains had made the roads too boggy, and she worried that perhaps she ought to bring her cashmere-lined gloves in case it should snow. Her uneasiness infected everyone, making even Lord Rushton fidget with his newspaper, until he snapped it open and almost tore it at the seam.

Finally, he laid down *The London Times,* drank the last of his coffee and rose, saying, "Well, we had best get a start so we may arrive while there is still light in the sky."

Lady Rushton rose as well, bustling from the room with instructions for the servants who were to stay and look after the townhouse. Already their maids and grooms and Lord Rushton's valet had gone ahead in one carriage, which was packed with most of their luggage.

Eleanor aided her mother by finding Evelyn's lost doll—it had fallen behind a trunk in the nursery. And by keeping herself out of the way of the bustle and excitement that flowed around her like a tumultuous river. All the while that card chafed against her skin.

She must hit upon something to ask for by the time they reached Westerley. Doing up the buttons of her fur-lined pelisse, she stepped out onto the front steps, her thoughts busy with cards and ideas.

Then she saw that he was there and every thought went straight out of her head.

The rain had stopped, and a bitter, chilling wind blew from the east, tossing aside the clouds so that patches of winter-sharp blue sky appeared between the billows of gray.

He stood on the bottom step, his tall beaver hat tucked under his arm and the wind playing delightful havoc with his golden hair, disordering it as if a lover's fingers ran through the silken strands. Next to him, a groom held the reins of a long-tailed gray—his horse, she knew at once, for the animal nosed his pockets, pushing playfully even as Geoffrey dug out a treat for the animal.

With an affectionate smile, he offered up a lump of sugar on the palm of his hand. "There you go, you greedy beast," he said, his voice warm. And then he stroked the gray's dark forelock, his face relaxed with boyish grace and a faint dimple beside his mouth.

Eleanor's heart turned over.

No. No. No. She did not want this. She was going to be sensible.

A lump rose in her throat and she looked away. This wasn't supposed to happen like this. She wanted to stamp her feet. She wanted to cry. She wanted to laugh aloud.

But most of all, she wanted to go to him and put her hand over his and smile up into his face and tell him that she was starting to fall in love with him.

Seven

Geoffrey glanced up to see Eleanor staring at him, a dazed look on her face and those enormous eyes fixed on him with an intent focus, as if she could see into his heart. Uncomfortable with that look, he tried for a smile and a small joke, and gestured to the two heavy carriages before the house. "Traveling light, I see."

He gave Donegal a pat, and started up the stairs towards her.

She blinked, put a hand up to straighten an already straight bonnet, and then said, her voice almost as sharp as the wind, as if his jest had somehow stirred her temper, "Did you expect a bride to come to you in nothing but her shift?"

He paused on the steps, and the image flashed into his mind then into his body—her wearing nothing but a near-transparent shift. Something dainty and as delicate as she. Something that revealed those curves now only hinted at. Something suited to a wedding night between lovers.

Heat rushed through him like fire through straw. As it did, her face reddened more than could be accounted for by the cold breeze. His stare trapped hers and he knew that same vision must have scorched her thoughts.

He sought for a light quip to ease the awareness that now stretched between them like a silken bond. But his usually glib tongue tangled. Instead of finding words, he found himself walking up the steps, drawn to her.

As he reached her side, her lips parted and she stared up at him, eyes wide. And he knew that what he really wanted to do was to add to that fierce blush warming her cheeks.

He wanted to kiss her.

He wanted to pull her towards him and find out if indeed that was a spark of invitation in her eyes.

He started to lean closer.

A booming male voice shook him from his intent. "Hullo, Staines. Shall we have more rain, do you think?"

Pulse still thudding, Geoff straightened and turned as Lord Rushton strode out of the house and onto the front steps. The rest of the Glover family seemed to spill out, and Geoff at once hammered down his impulses of a moment ago.

Devil take it, but he ought to have expected this from himself. He had done all he could these past few months to lust after the ladies, and he'd proven time and again that he was indeed damn near to a devil. And she was far too dainty a lady for him to come rutting after like a stallion after a mare in season. Which meant that after they wed, he had best keep his mistresses discreet and on the side so that she did not have to bear too much from him.

Lord, what a depressing life stretched out before him.

His glance slid back to Eleanor.

In the sharp air, her skin glowed. A stray wisp of seal-brown hair teased her cheek, and she brushed at it to no effect. His gaze traveled down her slender form, and his errant thoughts slipped back to images of her that he ought not to entertain while standing on a public thoroughfare.

Thankfully, Lord Rushton's booming voice rescued him once more from folly. "So, Staines, how far do you go with us?"

Geoff turned to settle the issue of traveling arrangements. He had decided that, as a courtesy, he would ride with Lord Rushton and his family until Kingston. One of Rushton's grooms could ride behind the coaches, leading Donegal. From Kingston, Geoff would ride ahead, so that he could be at Westerley to ensure all was ready for their welcome.

He told himself that it was no more than a matter of being polite to slow his own pace and travel with them. He was not, he repeated to himself, dragging his heels about going home. It did not matter that his last journey on this road had been one at breakneck speed away from Westerley. And it did not matter that he would be within walking distance of Cynthia again.

No. It did not matter. Not in the least.

And because it did not matter, he fixed his mind away from those fleeting memories of Cynthia that kept teasing his thoughts, and he watched Lord Rushton sort out who should ride in what coach.

Devil take it, but what a fuss five women could be.

Young Evelyn, it seemed, grew restless when she traveled, and so she would ride in the first carriage with Lord Rushton and Elizabeth, who knew best how to entertain the girl. That left Geoff to ride in the second carriage, with Eleanor, Emma, and Lady Rushton.

And so Geoff found himself sitting next to Eleanor, her shoulder pressed to his and her thigh brushing against his as the carriage rocked. She sat straight and still, and Geoff glanced at her occasionally, wondering if she was as aware of him as he was of her. It was odd, this tug of attraction, for she was not the least pretty. But still she drew his gaze, and he could only think it must be because of the contained puzzle she presented.

What was she thinking? Did she admire the view? Would she like Westerley? Her own family came from the Lake District, he knew, with its breathtaking scenery and vast distances. Would she appreciate the snug farm lands and the tidy villages around Guildford?

She tugged her bonnet ties as if she wanted to pull it off her head and . . . oh, but be damned, he had to stop thinking about taking off her garments.

His conversation was not much needed on the trip, for Miss Emma talked enough for everyone. She read to her mother from the traveling notes in *Cary's Itinerary,* pointing out Vauxhall and Battersea Rise as they passed. She also had a hundred questions about Westerley and how his family celebrated Christmas, which he answered with polite patience.

Lady Rushton swayed with the carriage, her eyes drifting shut as Emma droned on. Eleanor stared out the window, her gaze fixed on the winter-bare trees and brown, fallow farm lands.

He wanted to ask her a dozen questions, but her sister chattered in such a way that she could make a deaf man thankful for his affliction. For the first time since he had proposed marriage to Eleanor, Geoff thought that perhaps he had chosen well after all. He would have murdered pretty, charming, talkative Emma within a fortnight of being tied to her for life.

By the time the carriage pulled to a stop before The Castle in Kingston, Geoff was heartily glad to alight from the coach. He jumped out as soon as the door was open and before the grooms had let down the steps, and then he turned to hand the ladies out.

Eleanor glanced at him as he held her hand, her mouth curving in that mysterious, provoking smile of hers, but she said nothing to him of her thoughts as he steadied her descent.

While the ladies took tea in the best parlor, Geoff stayed long enough to drink a pint with Lord Rushton. The ale was strong and dark, and Geoff almost allowed himself to stay for a second. Finally, he had to admit to himself that now he really was postponing the inevitable.

He had to face the truth. He was going home. He would have to see both his father and Cynthia soon.

Not Cynthia, he told himself. She was now Mrs. Cheeverly, the vicar's wife.

What the devil would he say to her? Or she to him when next they met? But the perverse desire rose in him, as strong and bitter as the ale, that by bringing home his bride for her to meet, perhaps at last he would hurt her as much as she had hurt him.

"Which one's your bride, Geoff? Come and point her out so I do not kiss the wrong Glover girl."

Geoff came over to the window where Andrew stood, watching the Glovers arrive in a swirl of gowns, horses, carriages, and bustling servants in the green Westerley livery. The second-floor window faced east, to the front of the house and the graveled drive, where two crested coaches had pulled up to discharge their passengers and baggage. A leaden sky and the bare chestnut trees that lined the drive gave the scene a bleak look. *Or perhaps that's more my mood,* Geoffrey thought.

By rights, he ought to be downstairs to welcome his guests. However, he had wanted to change from his riding clothes, and to speak with his father. He had managed the former but not the latter, for his father's manservant had made it clear that the Earl had left word not to be disturbed until after Lord Rushton and his family arrived. Geoff knew better than to disobey one of his father's orders and risk the old man causing himself a seizure with his displeasure.

"That's her," Geoff said, easily spotting the still, blue-clad figure who stood beside the far carriage. "The invisible one."

"Has no one yet told her that brides are supposed to be the center of all attention?" Patrick said, strolling over to join them.

Geoff gave him a tight smile. "If you tell her that she may well disappear utterly. Eleanor is not fond of crowds."

Patrick lifted an eyebrow, but merely said, "Well, at least one of the Glover girls seems taken with the ancestral home."

Glancing down again, Geoff saw that Evelyn was gesturing up to the house, clutching her bonnet with her other hand as she leaned backwards to admire the building. She seemed to be exclaiming over the Jacobean brickwork, and Geoff had to smile at her show of enthusiasm which echoed his own deep love of the house.

He had not realized how much he had missed Westerley over the past nine months until he saw it again. And now he was sorry that he had allowed memories of Cynthia to keep him away so long. However, all that was done with. And ought to be put away.

Turning his attention to his bride-to-be, Geoff wondered if her eyes, too, glowed with delight, or if she regarded her future home with displeasure. But he found that she had vanished. Completely this time.

Disappointment stirred inside him. And a pang of guilt. He should be in the hall, smiling and offering Westerley's hospitality. She had been so silent earlier. Perhaps she was dreading this? Or nervous at meeting his father? Heavens knew, most people had that reaction to the Earl of Herndon, for he had a well-earned reputation, even from the sickbed, of having a tongue as sharp as a headsman's ax.

Suddenly, Geoff wanted to let Eleanor know that she would find a home here. He wanted to put that shy smile back into her eyes.

Turning on his heel, he started for the stairs, saying to his brothers, "Come on, you laggards. We have guests to attend."

* * *

Eleanor had fallen in love. Deeply. Passionately. Desperately. She had expected Westerley to be some grand house, daunting and aged, large and domineering—something suitable to the Earl of Herndon. Instead she had taken one look up at the time-aged brickwork, at the careful additions to the house that balanced the main hall with rebuilt and tidy wings, at the mullioned windows and the elegant proportions.

Home. My home now.

She knew she could live here.

Inside the cavernous main hall, the Westerley butler—Bellows, as he introduced himself—took charge, directing footmen to assist with the luggage and maids to take wraps. Eleanor handed over her bonnet and her gloves, and then wandered the hall, taking it all in, still pleased and hugging that pleasure inside herself.

The hall was ancient. The stone floor, vast space, and huge hearth set with a cheerful fire told of its once having been the manor hall where past earls dispensed local justice and law to the land. But some earl interested in his own comfort had plastered the walls and painted them a soft cream, and tapestries now hung beside the ancient fireplace. Thick, oriental carpets softened the room and were strewn on the floor in comfortable disarray.

A stairway took up most of the fourth wall, and as Evelyn and Emma flitted around the room to admire the suits of armor placed against either side of the front entrance, the others went to warm themselves by the hearth fire. But Eleanor stopped opposite the fire, before a life-size painting of what she assumed must be the current earl.

Dressed in the cuffed and skirted coat of the last century, with his brown hair tied back, the man stood beside a chestnut horse, one hand on the reins as if he was about to turn and swing up into the saddle. He held a tricorn hat in his other hand. In the background, a hunt crossed a hillside, the horses' legs stretched out in full gallop, following running hounds.

Both horse and master looked stiff and awkward, but the painter had caught in the man's blue eyes an intensity of personality that reminded Eleanor strongly of how Lord Staines could look when something displeased him. She gathered, from the man's expression, that he had not enjoyed standing for his portrait.

A shiver chased down her spine. This looked to be an uncomfortable man, demanding and domineering, and not at all an easy sort of father-in-law. But perhaps age and sickness had softened his manner.

And then Lord Staines's voice carried to her, and with a sense of relief she turned to see him coming down the great stairs that stood opposite the front doors.

"Welcome to Westerley. Forgive me for not being here to greet you sooner."

He came downstairs, his brothers behind him, and Eleanor was pleased to note that Westerley suited him. He looked . . . well, he looked as homelike as this house.

In country clothes—a faded brown jacket, breeches and boots, a buff waistcoat and casually tied white cravat—he could almost be taken for a local squire. Of course, he still had those impossible good looks. But she decided she liked him a little rumpled like this, for she did not feel so horribly aware of her own flaws.

And then she realized he was saying something to her father, and looking at her. ". . . in fact, I should like to take Eleanor up to meet my father now."

A moment's panic flared in Eleanor. Meet Lord Herndon? Now? With her curls flattened by her bonnet, and her skirts crushed from sitting too long in a carriage?

Before she could protest, Lord Staines offered his arm, and Eleanor glanced at her mother, who gave her a look that plainly said, "Well, go on."

So she came forward and laid her hand upon his arm, and started up the stairs with him.

As they moved away from the others, he said to her, a dry tone softening his words, "He's a dreadful bully, but he will like you better if you don't let him frighten you. And don't be alarmed if he seems ready to expire at any second. He has been like that for years. He has said he will live to see me wed, and he is a man who keeps his vows."

Apprehension tightened Eleanor's face. How could a dying man—and one who had been dying for so long—be such a bully? She thought back to that stern face from the portrait and those hard, blue eyes. Why could she have not met him after dinner and a few glasses of wine to fortify her nerves?

She wondered if she should ask about the Earl's health, but that seemed apt to stir painful feelings, so instead she asked about the house—when it had been built, and how many rooms it had.

The topic proved a good one, for Lord Staines seemed to relax and as he spoke, Eleanor smiled to herself to hear the pride and affection that lay in his voice. He pointed out features of the house—the *trompe l'oeil* details on the staircase, the Italian influence brought to the house by his great-grandfather. And he introduced her to various ancestral portraits, almost all of which included a horse or a dog.

"If you like, and if the weather holds good, we could ride over the grounds tomorrow or the day after. There is not much to see, this time of year. But we also hold a Christmas hunt, which is quite the local event. You might enjoy that."

"Do you hunt very much?" she asked, a little dismayed.

He glanced down at her. A frown drew his brows together and then his face relaxed again. "Let me guess—your sympathies are more with the fox than with the hounds?"

Color warmed her cheeks and throat, but she met his stare, a little irked by the fact that he looked ready to humor her about this. "Yes, they do. Poor animals. How should you like to be chased by a pack of barking, baying beasts three times your size, and run ragged 'til you must go to earth and face your death at the end of their fangs?"

She glared at him, but his eyes only glinted warmer.

"I supposed I should not like that at all, but you might spare a thought for the farmer's poor hens who face a similar fate, only from the fangs of that same innocent fox you champion."

She would have argued the point, for she thought it quite possible to keep foxes from hen houses with proper construction, only he stopped before a set of oak doors and the amusement left his face.

"And now I would urge you to leave behind your sympathies with the hunted. My father was a rather passionate huntsman in his day and will not find such sentiments at all endearing."

She thought back to the portrait of his father, and of all the other family paintings with hunting dogs and horses. Oh, dear, she was marrying into a sporting family. She had not given it much thought in London, for in a family of girls, it had never been much of a topic. But now the thought of Lord Staines coming home to her, blood on his hands from shooting birds and hunting foxes left her queasy.

Feeling slightly ill, she watched as Lord Staines reached for the door knob, and she almost reached out to stop him, to tell him this was all such a mistake, that they were mismatched and would never suit.

Only before she could move or say anything, the door swung open inwards, and an elderly man, stocky and dressed in a crooked white wig and old-fashioned black breeches and coat, stepped into the hallway with them. His watery blue-gray eyes registered surprise, and then he frowned fiercely at them, his heavy jowls dragging down.

For an instant Eleanor wondered if he could be Lord

Herndon, but he looked nothing like the man in the portrait, and nothing like Lord Staines.

"Ibbottson?" Staines said, puzzlement in his voice. "I had not heard you'd been summoned." Eleanor felt tension tighten his arm under her touch. "Good God, he is not . . ."

"No, he is not," the thick-set elderly man snapped, his voice deep and gravely. A sheaf of papers crumpled in his hands. "A doctor may see his patient, I should hope, and not have the world thinking it is his last call."

Tension eased from Staines's shoulders, but Geoff was left wondering why he had not been told of the doctor's visit.

Ibbottson seemed as aware of the breech in protocol, for he shifted on his feet, and then offered by way of explaining his presence, "Lord Herndon has taken an interest in the hospital I have proposed to build. He may offer an endowment for it."

Startled, Geoff stared at the man. His father funding a hospital? Despite his own illness, the Earl had always shown the greatest scorn for the weak and the sickly. He had put himself back in his own bed, in fact, numerous times by overestimating his own strength, but his obstinate will seemed to drive him to cling to life. However, perhaps with his own mortality so close, he had realized that, for some, weakness could not be overcome.

"What a kind thing to do," Eleanor said, her voice soft.

Geoff glanced down at her. He had almost forgotten her presence, and now her words pulled a crooked smile from him. "Kind" was not a word to associate with the Earl of Herndon. She would soon enough learn that.

Clearing his throat, Ibbottson's deep jowls dragged into a heavy scowl. "Well, Staines, do you present me, or wish to keep me a family secret?"

"Your pardon. Miss Eleanor Glover, this is Dr. Ibbottson, who has looked after us far longer than we deserve. Dr. Ibbottson, this is my wife-to-be."

A light flickered at the back of Dr. Ibbottson's watery eyes as he glanced at Eleanor, and Geoff had the oddest feeling that the man looked guilty about something. Lord, was he keeping it secret that the Earl was in worse condition than his letter had hinted? It would be very like the Earl to demand that Ibbottson keep silent—and, as a doctor, Ibbottson would be bound to keep such a confidence.

Fear tightened inside Geoff, and his hands chilled. Ancient memories of his mother's death—the abruptness of it, the fracture it had left in the family, the hole it had carved inside him—started to crawl loose. He shut them off, pushing them ruthlessly aside and locking them away.

Ibbottson was saying something to Eleanor, something about wishing her well and that she must look upon him as an old friend if she ever needed anyone. Geoff scowled. The man's tone sounded so grim that he could be mistaken for comforting the fatally doomed, not congratulating a bride.

"You will stay to dinner?" Geoff asked, his words abrupt. He wanted time to sit with the man and see what he could pry out of the fellow about his father's true condition.

That look flickered at the back of Ibbottson's eyes again, and he shifted on his feet, as if his own weight was too much for him to carry. "Thank you, no. Mrs. Patterson is expecting her third child, and I promised to call upon her today."

"Then tomorrow?" Geoff said, determined. As a precaution against the whims of fate, he had purchased a Special License so that he and Eleanor could marry when and where they chose, and not be bound by the laws that kept weddings to morning hours and sanctioned churches. He would prefer not having to rush this affair—was it not already approaching too fast? However, if his father's condition had worsened, he would put forward the wedding to this very afternoon if need be.

Ibbottson had been muttering about patients to see, and

the uncertain weather, and not at all acting as if the Earl was about to expire.

And then Eleanor, her voice shy, added, "Please do come, sir. Is it not a season to share warmth and good spirits?"

Geoff glanced down at her. She had lowered her chin, but she gave the doctor a charming smile that curved her lips and warmed her eyes. With a slight shock, Geoff realized that when she chose to focus that smile of hers upon a fellow it wove a potent allure. The doctor stammered a response, but bowed and gave way before her.

And why the devil has she never turned that particular look upon me? Geoff thought with a scowl.

With another bow, the doctor took his leave.

Eleanor kept her smile in place as she glanced back to Geoff, but the charm she had directed to the doctor was already fading. That irritated him, and it irritated him even more that he cared. After all, what the devil right did he have to demand anything from her? He had set out his terms for a marriage, and now he only waited to hear her terms on that damnable card. And hear them he would. Soon, he vowed.

Opening the door, he swept his arm out for her to enter before him, and he said, meaning to keep his voice light, but unable to keep a touch of irritation from his tone, "Save some of those feminine wiles of yours for my father."

She shot him a puzzled glance, but then she went into the room. Taking a deep breath, Geoff followed, feeling all too like Daniel entering the lion's den.

And he hoped like the devil that the Earl was in a decent mood and on his best behavior, or poor Eleanor might well decide she would do better not to marry into this family after all.

Eight

Eleanor entered a dark, cavernous room. Her courage faltered and she fingered her high-waisted wool gown and wished she had changed into something better than a creased traveling dress. However, the touch of Lord Staines's—Geoffrey's hand—at her back kept her moving forward into the gloom.

Outside, winter had robbed all but a faint haze of light from the leaden sky. It might as well have been midnight in this room. On the far wall, a brace of candles glowed on a side table. Two more candles in wall sconces illuminated wine-colored wall hangings and pooled light around an enormous, carved mahogany four-poster bed, hung with velvet bed curtains. To her left, a meager fire in the hearth looked as if it, too, had had its spirits dampened by the gloom.

Thankfully, the room smelled of spices and tobacco. She had dreaded visiting her own grandfather when he lay dying, for he had smelled of sickness and old man, and of death.

As she moved forward—her boots silenced by the thick rugs—she noted the heavy, old fashioned furnishings that loomed up from the shadows as if they had been forgotten here. What a wonderful room for fancy dress, for men in cavalier curls, and women in low-cut lace and Queen Anne brocades.

Then her wandering gaze came to rest on the Earl of Herndon.

The Earl lay on his bed, motionless, his eyes closed. His shrunken body lay wrapped in fine lawn and a rich purple brocade robe. Wisps of white hair poked out like cotton from under a nightcap of white linen. His hand lay on the sheet that covered him, and on his finger, a huge ruby glinted in the candlelight.

Just as she began to wonder if the doctor had been too quick to leave his patient's side, the Earl's eyes popped open. Eleanor nearly jumped out of her skin.

"Who is it?" the Earl demanded, his voice far stronger than his appearance would lead anyone to believe. Ice-blue eyes fixed on her, skewering her with their glare.

"I've brought my wife-to-be to meet you," Lord Staines said, moving forward into the candlelight and bringing Eleanor with him.

"Who?" The Earl's right hand, which lay on the covers, shook slightly, and Eleanor stared at the wrinkled and age-spotted skin that stretched over long fingers and a wide-backed hand. "Help me sit up," the Earl ordered, as if his son were a servant.

Calmly, Lord Staines replied, "You may help yourself, sir, or you may stay as you are. I am going to help Eleanor to a chair."

Shocked by this seemingly callous treatment of his father, Eleanor turned to protest. But Staines had already dragged up one of those monstrous chairs, as if it were as light as a footstool. She turned back to offer her own assistance to the Earl, but he had indeed propped himself up in the bed without any aid.

Confused, she sat down in the high-backed chair, remembering that Lord Staines had said something about how she was supposed to act with his father. Only she couldn't remember what his advice had been. Folding her cold fingers together, she waited to see what would happen next.

The Earl stared at her, his white eyebrows bunched together, those impossibly blue eyes snapping fire like the finest sapphires. He did indeed have his son's eyes—or rather, Lord Staines had his eyes from his father.

"So, who is she?" the Earl snapped, narrowing his eyes as if he found it difficult to see. Or perhaps because he disapproved of what he saw.

A touch of irritation rose in her. She was used to being overlooked, but not to being discussed as if she were not in the room at all. "I am Eleanor. Lord Rushton's daughter."

"I know you're one of Edward's gels. Didn't I swear to him one of my boys would marry one of you? With four of you—and three boys myself—why not?"

She could not think of an answer to that.

The Earl did not wait for her to answer, but demanded, "So, which are you? You're not the eldest. She's said to be a beauty, or did the gossips get that wrong?"

"Father," Staines interrupted, his voice mild, but also with a touch of warning in his tone. "Do you wish a wedding, or to have me a rejected suitor?"

"Nonsense. She's got your ring."

Eleanor glanced down at her bare hands. "Well, actually . . ."

"What? No ring to pledge her? Oh, my sweet Amanda, what sons you gave me." The old man rolled his eyes, and clutched at his chest with a trembling hand.

Instinctively, Eleanor started to rise to go to him, but a hard grip on her shoulder stayed her. She turned to look up at Lord Staines, to see if he had held her back so that he could go to his father. But he stood next to her, frowning, his eyes narrowed, his body taut. Did he have no care for his father's health? But he must. She had noticed the distress in his eyes when he had spoken to the doctor. And she could not now mistake the tension that flowed into her from his touch.

But why then did he not go to the Earl's side?

Geoffrey glanced down at Eleanor's pale, worried face. Lord, she looked a Madonna, with the light falling on her oval face and the rest of her in shadows. However, he knew quite well that this was a test for her—his father was looking for signs of weakness. For signs that she was too feeling, too sensitive. He had seen the Earl do this with other relatives. And, to be honest, having his father try his tricks was the best sign he could have asked to have seen. The Earl could not be too close to death if he could still think to make others do his bidding by any means, fair or foul.

His tone intentionally dry, Geoff asked, "Father, I would ask you to bid welcome to Eleanor, and then I will take her off to look over Mother's rings and see if any of them suit her. And if they do not, I shall buy her one in Guildford before Christmas comes."

The Earl's eyes opened a slit. He gave his son a hard, assessing stare. No, the lad wasn't going to rise to the lure. He could have chuckled at his son's sense and strength, but that was not something a dying man did. So he glanced at the girl. Staines wasn't going to let her jump though any hoops either. But she wanted to. He saw it in the softness in her eyes. In the way she leaned forward against Staines's restraining hand. Bloody all, but he would indeed turn up his toes and have done with it if his son had another fainting lily of a girl.

"I buried your mother with her ring," he said, opening his eyes, and daring his son to offer to open the family vault. He had indeed buried his Amanda with the emerald he had given her—an heirloom that had been in the family since before the Conquest. But he would have thrown the damn thing in the Wey if it would have brought his Amanda back to him.

"Then I shan't trouble her for it," Staines said, unruffled. "There must be a dozen others the family has collected. Come, now, and bid Eleanor a civil good-day, father. Or I won't bring her back to see you again."

For an instant, anger kindled in the Earl. Damn, arrogant pup. Did he think he wore the title already? He glared at his eldest, and the boy matched his stare with one just as haughty and twice as indifferent. He gave a cackle of laugher then, and covered it with a raspy cough, and used his shaking hand over his mouth for good measure.

Glancing up, he saw that Staines remained unmoved and unmoving. But that Glover girl had gone all soft and would have been jumping to his bidding if Staines had allowed it.

She wasn't going to do. Not at all. Bloody all! He'd have to do something about her it seemed.

He waved at them with his shaking hand, slumping back down in his bed. "You're arrogant, boy. But it'll serve you well when you have to wear my coronet. Now, you, gel, come here and give your soon-to-be father a kiss."

The girl froze for an instant, and the Earl wondered if he could frighten her into crying off this marriage. He'd wager that he could. He'd find her weakness, and get her swapped for one of her sisters, if any of them had any proper spine in 'em.

She glanced up at Staines once, her eyes huge in her face. Staines's hand relaxed on her shoulder and he gave a small nod.

Ten to one, she makes an excuse not to, the Earl thought.

But she surprised him by rising and moving to the bedside. He could see the pulse beating in her throat, but her hands didn't quiver even as she covered his damned palsied one.

Leaning down, she brushed her lips to his cheek. He peered into her face, studying it, wondering if his first impression had been wrong, wishing Staines would go away and let him have at her on his own.

"Not much like my Amanda," he muttered, weighing her. No beauty. No height. But there was something at the back of those dark eyes. Damn, but he wished he could see her better. He would just have to corner her on his own and see if he could take her apart to see if she could breed him strong grandsons or not.

Rousing himself, the Earl glared at his eldest son. "Take her off, boy. Find her a ring."

Geoffrey gave his father a dutiful bow. "Yes, my lord," he said, irony heavy in his dulcet tone. The Earl gave another chuckle, and Geoffrey relaxed muscles in his shoulders that he had not known to be tense. He took Eleanor out of the room before his father's mood changed. All taken together, it had gone well. Now if only he could continue to spare Eleanor the worst side of his father's manipulations, there might still be a Christmas wedding.

Stepping out into the hallway, Eleanor blinked. She looked a little dazed, and Geoff could only think that she had done well not to run from the room. Herndon had certainly reduced more than one of his female relatives to tears after luring them into trying to help him, and then verbally cutting them apart.

When the door was shut behind him, he turned to her. "We do not have to look for a ring just now. Would you rather go to your room and rest? There is, after all, a good fortnight to Christmas."

At the mention of that short time, Eleanor's face turned even more ashen and he could sympathize. Fourteen days until they married. It sounded ominously near.

* * *

Eleanor decided she had never had such an encounter before. Was the Earl a dying man, or an invalid who used his illness more like a weapon than a curse? Lord Staines had seemed concerned enough about his father when he spoke to Dr. Ibbottson. But he had not acted as if he cared in the least for his father. Was he a cold-hearted man who did not care, or a wounded one who could not show that he cared? Or a cautious man who knew better than to jump to his father's orders?

All of it was just too confusing.

Rising from her bed where she had lain down before dressing for dinner, Eleanor went to the writing desk in her room. Lord Staines had taken her to a charming room that overlooked the back of the house to the west. The twilight sky showed nothing of the view outside, but the room was done up in cheerful soft yellows, with a bright fire in the hearth and candles enough to hold back the winter's gloom.

Lord Staines had shown her every courtesy, asking her to make use of the house as if she were already its mistress. But Eleanor felt more awkward and out-of-place than she ever had in her life.

Why did the man have to ask to marry me? she thought, feeling cross and tired and faintly irritable. *Why could he not have asked Emma? She would adore being a countess.* But Emma really was only sixteen, too young to marry, and the stubborn thought persisted in the back of Eleanor's mind that if someone had a magic wand to wave which would remove Lord Staines's proposal, Eleanor would break that wand over her knee.

The sad truth was that she did not want to give him up, but she did not know what to do with him either.

Sitting down at the rosewood table that stood before the curtained windows with their gold drapes, she took his card from her sleeve.

Geoffrey Frederick Westerley, Viscount Staines, read the careful script.

She turned it over and stared at the very white and very empty back of it. Then she picked up the quill and opened the ink pot. She had promised herself to come up with something to write before she reached Westerley. And she had had some excellent ideas. She could ask for a honeymoon trip to . . . well, to someplace exotic, although she had no particular wish to travel. But it sounded good. Better still, she could ask to set up her own charity. Only she could think of no specific cause to champion.

With a sigh, she let her mind wander. She drew swirls in the corner of the card. And then drew a pansy. She dipped her quill again, and waited for inspiration.

Her mind drifted until a soft knock on the door and an inquiry from one of the Westerley maids reminded her that it was time to dress for dinner.

She glanced down at the card, and her eyes widened with horror. Her hand had been straying along with her thoughts and she had written something she never could show to Lord Staines.

Dipping her quill again, she blotted ink across the word she had written, crossing it out again and again until only a black stain remained. Then she thrust the card into the stationery she had brought with her. Rising, she called to her maid so that she could dress and dine, and she vowed to forget about what she had put down on that wretched card.

"You saw them at dinner. What are we going to do to help?" Emma said. Pulling her dressing gown tighter around her, she tucked her slippered feet more firmly under one of Elizabeth's pillows. Westerley could be a cold, drafty house at night.

Across from her, with her back against one of the four

posts on Elizabeth's bed, Evelyn made a face. "I thought Lord Staines treated everyone very well. He even told a funny story about trying to bring home the Yule log by himself one year, and rolling it down a hill and through the drawing room windows."

Evelyn twisted, forcing Elizabeth, who was brushing her younger sister's hair, to pause. "Do you think he shall find us a Yule log this year big enough to crash down the front doors of the house?"

Smiling, Elizabeth started to answer, but Emma's voice cut off her reply. "We are here to speak of helping Eleanor, not Yule logs, and if you cannot keep to that topic, then you ought to go to bed."

Evelyn made a face at her sister, but Elizabeth said, worry etched in her soft voice, "What if Eleanor does not want our help?"

Scowling, Emma grabbed a pillow and hugged it. "We are not speaking of wants, we are discussing needs, particularly the need to ensure Eleanor's happiness in a marriage in which she is loved."

Evelyn gave a rude snort, then said, "But of course he will love her. How could anyone not love Ellie?"

Elizabeth stopped brushing Evelyn's dark brown hair, and Emma exchanged an exasperated look with her over their younger sister's head. Emma let out a sigh. She had known tonight that it was time to take a helping hand in this matter. She had seen over the short time of Eleanor's engagement how her sister looked at Lord Staines—with her heart in her eyes. And she knew, down to her bones, that if Eleanor married without love, well, they might as well simply take food, water, and air from her as well. For what woman did not need love?

Pushing aside the pillow, Emma sat up straighter. "I am not saying we have to do very much. Just . . . help a touch. It is the season of love and good will, so that should aid us. But if Lord Staines is not given the chance to really know Ellie, how can he possibly come to love her?"

"And if he starts to know her and does not love her?" Elizabeth asked, the silver-backed brush held still in her hand and her voice tensed.

"Well, better that Ellie should know that before they are wed rather than after, when it is too late to do anything about it."

"It already seems too late," Elizabeth said, and then she sat down on the bed and stared at the brush in her hand.

"Rubbish," Evelyn said, and glared back unrepentant when her sisters frowned at her.

Elizabeth shook her head. "Really, Evelyn. Your language."

"That is not the topic in discussion," Evelyn said, her chin up and starting to braid her long hair. "It is Ellie we are helping. So what must we do?"

Sitting forward, Emma smiled. "It is simple, really. We must offer Ellie more opportunity to be with Lord Staines. Alone. After all, how could he not fall in love with our Ellie once he realizes how sweet and kind she is?"

Elizabeth started to say that it was quite possible for men to fall in love for many reasons, none of them having to do with sweetness or kindness. However, Evelyn leaned forward, eager-eyed to agree with Emma. Elizabeth glanced from one sister to the other, and decided it would hurt nothing for Lord Staines and Eleanor to become better acquainted. But, oh, how she wished her Captain Singleton was here to give her a gentleman's point-of-view.

But he was not, and so she joined her sisters in starting to make plans for how they could more often throw Eleanor and Lord Staines together, even as she worried that this was not enough to help Eleanor avoid making a mistake with this arranged marriage.

In another part of Westerley, a similar council of war had convened.

Patrick and Andrew Westerley stood in the billiards room, their coats off, their waistcoats unbuttoned and their cravats tugged loose. The fire in the hearth lay in dying coals and embers, but fresh candles in the wall sconces gave plenty of light for their play, while a full decanter of brandy stood open on a side table beside two crystal goblets.

Silent and concentrating, Andrew circled the table, eyeing the possible shots. Patrick stared into the dying fire, nursing his brandy, his eyes darkened with thoughts and one dark lock of hair falling forward on his brow to curl over his left eye.

Just as Andrew had lined up his cue on his target, Patrick turned. "We have to do something."

Andrew's hands tightened on his cue and his shot went wide. He glanced up at his brother, and wished that it were still possible to thump the fellow. But Patrick had always been fast, and now he was tall and broad in the shoulder. Not a good idea to try and thump a fellow who might thump back even harder.

Leaning on his cue stick, Andrew took up his own drink and downed a warming gulp. "So you keep saying, but you have yet to say what we must do."

Patrick set down his brandy and came around the table to take his shot. "Affairs of the heart are supposed to be your territory, vicar."

"I am not a vicar, yet. And this is about the least hearty affair I've ever seen. And Geoff will not welcome our interference if he learns of it."

Patrick made his shot, then straightened. "You are indeed a man of cloth—cloth-headedness. The trick of it is to make certain Geoff don't learn about it. And if we do not help Geoff through the next two weeks, who will?"

Andrew started to circle the table, looking for his next shot. "Geoff wants this all proper and right."

"Yes, I know. I saw him tonight, polite as a nun."

"Painfully so."

"Exactly. How long do you think he can keep that up?"

Andrew frowned. Much as he hated to admit it, his brother had a point. Geoff could do the proper, but he had a fuse as short as their sire's. Geoff was a man to get things done, whether they wanted getting done or not. The strain of entertaining the Glovers, of trying to keep all reasonable, was bound to tell on him.

Growing up in a house without a mother and with their father often ill, it had been Geoff who had managed things. He had measured out the discipline and the praise and most of the lessons. They owed him much.

And what, after all, would Lord Rushton think, if Geoff ripped up at Eleanor over something? It might not happen, but then again it might.

Andrew made his shot, pocketed a ball, and he moved to make his next shot. "What do you suggest?"

He missed his shot and straightened as Patrick came around the table. Instead of taking his turn, Patrick leaned on his cue, his eyes only the slightest bit heavy from drink and the late hour.

"I'm not saying we do anything to interfere in Geoff's choice of bride. Just that we offer a little buffer to keep him and his intended from seeing more of each other than is good before a marriage. Dovecott married his bride with no more than a day spent with her, and look how well that's turned out."

"Dovecott is an idiot."

"Yes, but a happy idiot. And just how happy do you think Geoff would be if this girl takes a shunner to him? We've both agreed that he cannot go though what Cynthia put him through again."

Andrew scowled. "I am not certain this would be at all the same. He was in love with Cynthia. Now, will you finish the game? It is your shot."

Hefting his cue, Patrick made his shot—and then another and another, rapidly clearing the table. Then he racked his cue. "That's fifty quid you owe me, brother. And while Geoff may not love his bride, he's still a man with pride."

Racking his own cue, Andrew eyed his brother. He drank back his brandy and then said, "You know, of course, that it is going to be damn hard to keep Geoff from spending too much time with his intended when we have a house full of Glover ladies and the season of celebration upon us."

Patrick clapped a hand on his brother's shoulder. "My dear fellow, the day that I cannot occupy the attention of three ladies, one of them a schoolgirl, that is the day you may see me in my grave. Which leaves you well able to occupy Miss Eleanor's time. And then we shall all have a happy Christmas, and be able to wish our brother well on his wedding day."

Geoffrey came downstairs the next morning to find his brothers in a suspiciously cheerful mood. The Glovers were downstairs to breakfast already, and he greeted them, and then sat down to drink his coffee and watch his brothers entertain everyone. Patrick was full of amusing political stories, and Andrew seemed to be monopolizing Eleanor's time, Geoff thought, a touch of irritation lacing through him.

Devil take it, what had Andrew said to her to make her smile that warmly? And how had he gotten her to talk so much? He wanted to know, but with Andrew on one side of her, and Patrick on the other, and her sisters and family surrounding them, Geoff had no choice but to sit at the far end of the table and bide his time.

At last she rose and glanced shyly up at him. He rose as well, his now cold coffee forgotten. "Would you care to pick out your ring now?"

"Ring?" Patrick said, rising. "Excellent idea, Geoff. A shopping expedition to Guildford to get a ring. And I'm certain the Misses Glover would like to do some Christmas shopping. We have a tradition at Westerley of exchanging gifts on Christmas Eve, you know," he said, glancing down to the glowing eyes of Emma and Evelyn Glover.

"Oh, may we, Mama?" Emma said, turning to her mother. "May we go shopping in Guildford?"

Lady Rushton looked uncertain, but Lord Rushton chuckled and said, "Best take a pair of footmen with you to carry all the packages."

With that, Eleanor found herself swept into a shopping expedition. She glanced at Lord Staines as plans were made by his brothers and her sisters, and she had the fleeting impression that this was not what he had had in mind when he had asked her about a ring. He had offered to allow her to choose a ring from the Westerley jewels, and she could not decide if she preferred a ring all her own, or something that had long been in his family. But the choice did not seem to be hers anyway.

Her sisters took her away to dress for the weather—for while the sun had come out, frost lay on the ground and a sharp wind blew from the northeast.

Within all too short a time, the carriages were at the door, and she was helped into a coach, but not by Lord Staines.

His brother, Andrew, claimed the honor of assisting her. And with a smile, he took her hand and guided her to the forward coach. She had only time to glance back at Lord Staines, and to see the scowl on his face. For an instant, it flashed into her mind that he was jealous. But that was absurd. Jealous of what? It must be that he did not want to go to Guildford. Yes, that made sense. He wanted her to choose a ring from those in his family.

And she determined then and there not to like any rings in Guildford.

It turned out to be easier than she expected to keep to her resolve. Lord Staines disliked all the rings to be had at Findlay and Firth's, the main jewelers on Guildford's High Street. He waved away the diamonds, which he found too small and colorless. Eleanor let out a relieved breath at that, for she thought the same thing.

But Lord Staines found the rubies too cloudy, the sapphires lacking the true violet color of an excellent stone, and the emeralds—which Eleanor actually preferred—to have too plain a setting. Mr. Findlay, desperate to please, offered a tray of less precious stones—topaz, aquamarine, garnets, and pearls. But Lord Staines scorned them as unsuitable for his future countess.

"Have you nothing else?" he asked.

Eleanor rose from her chair and began to wander the shop. Emma and Evelyn, restless and bored with the task of selecting a ring had already dragged away Lord Staines's youngest brother, Patrick, taking him with them to show them Guildford, and taking Lady Rushton with them as well. They had promised to meet up at The Rose for refreshments before they returned to Westerley. Now Elizabeth had coaxed Andrew Westerley into helping her choose a watch fob as a present for her father.

Poor Mr. Westerley, Eleanor thought, as Elizabeth asked to see tray upon tray of fobs, and then sought his opinion on each. *He doesn't want to be here either.*

Then the door to the shop opened with a gust of cold air and a tinkling of the bell that hung from the door.

Eleanor turned and saw framed in the doorway one of the most beautiful women she had ever seen in her life.

Golden curls peeked out from a green velvet bonnet that was lined with a cream satin that perfectly matched the cream of her skin. The curls and bonnet framed a heart-shaped face as perfect and symmetrical as any Eleanor had ever seen. She caught her breath at such beauty. Eyebrows and lashes of darker gold lined wide, pale silver-gray eyes.

The green velvet of the lady's cloak lay back over one shoulder to reveal a graceful, slim figure.

Eleanor turned, thinking to remark to Elizabeth on the lady's beauty. But as she turned, she caught sight of Lord Staines's face. Her heart tightened at the wretched misery etched into deep lines around his mouth and across his forehead.

That wounded look was back in his eyes, as sharp and clear as shards of shattered crystal. And the sight of this beautiful woman had put it there.

Nine

The hole inside him opened again, the one he had spent the last nine months filling with drink and other women and anything to obliterate her image. And the last strand of hope snapped like a cut string.

What a fool he had been, he thought bitterly, disgusted with himself. He had allowed himself to believe in the fantasy of how he had wanted this meeting to go. He had pictured the regret that would cloud her eyes and the smile she would offer. He had imagined how his arms would enfold her, and the lemon and spice and woman scent of her, teasing and familiar, would encircle him, and she would say at last that she loved him.

But the illusion that she might ever open her heart to him vanished in that small step she took backwards.

She looked down and then away, as if seeking some escape. Anguish rose up from his chest and flooded his throat, almost choking him. She regretted nothing, had forgotten nothing. He still frightened her.

He wanted to die.

Manners saved him.

He must be polite. Introduce everyone. He had to bow and smile, and he would be damned to hell before he showed any of the raw agony and simmering anger that swirled in him in a poisonous blend. He wanted to slam his hand into something. Instead, he bowed. He wanted to take hold of her and force her to realize that he loved her. Instead, he clenched his jaw, and then smiled and did what was expected of him, a lord, an earl's son, a gentleman who had been rejected by the woman he adored.

"Mrs. Cheeverly, it has been some time," he said, his voice sounding strained and hollow to himself. He turned away from her. It hurt to look at her and not be able to touch her.

"Miss Glover and Miss Eleanor Glover," he went on, still civil and in control. "This is Mrs. Cynthia Cheeverly. . . ." *the woman I love—but cannot have.* He did not say the words but they echoed inside him like stones down an endless well.

The ladies exchanged stares as if the words he had not spoken lay in the air between them, visible as white paint. He watched Eleanor and Cynthia eye each other, his heart still tangled with his head, and all of him ached with bitter, hopeless regrets.

Why the devil did I not elope to Scotland and take my bride anywhere else in the world?

But he knew the answer. Those damned hopes had snared him, trapping him into this. That and his promises to his father to bring his bride to Westerley and marry there. He'd had no choice about this.

Cynthia came forward, graceful and gracious as ever, her voice melodic and only a little shy as she shook hands with the other ladies. His gaze devoured her, as if he had been released from prison into sunlight and fresh air for the first time in years.

Look, but do not touch. She never wanted your touch.

Devil a bit, but how was he supposed to get through a wedding ceremony and this Christmas smiling with good cheer when what he wanted to do was act a savage, surly brute?

A soft touch on his arm drew his glance down to Eleanor.

"Please, I hate to be rude, but may we leave? I have the most awful headache. Shopping sometimes does that, I fear."

In truth, Eleanor felt fine, other than for the sick churning in her stomach. That awful look had come back to Lord Staines's eyes, and she had also noted the recognition in Mrs. Cynthia Cheeverly's eyes. She had watched enough of the London world to know when two people shared an intimate past and were both made uncomfortable by it. And her only thought was: *How do I get him from this place before he cannot bear it any longer?*

She did not understand what had come between these two, but she could see that whatever it was still had the power to wound. And she only wanted to get him away from here.

In his glance at her, Eleanor could see relief flicker in his eyes for an instant. Then it vanished as his mask and control fell into place. Ah, but she had done the right thing to offer him an escape. Him and herself.

He offered apologies, led the ladies to the door, but then a man, thin, dressed in sober black stepped through the entrance. "Cynthia, my dear, I forgot . . ."

What he forgot stopped on his tongue as his glance took in Lord Staines and the ladies. He swept off his tall black hat and a smile lifted his thin mouth.

He had a narrow face and body, thinning brown hair, and vague brown eyes. His shoulders sloped slightly, and he dressed with precise neatness. He looked a man with no dangerous, hidden depths. A man with no raw passions simmering in blazing eyes. In fact, he could not look more opposite, Eleanor thought, from the man who stood beside her.

"Staines, well met, and greetings of this happy season. I see, Cynthia, that you have already exchanged a welcome with your old playmate." He gave a warm smile to his wife, as if inviting her to tell him that he had just made a most excellent joke.

Eleanor felt the tension in Lord Staines bleed into her, filling her mind, tightening her nerves, until she wanted to shift from foot to foot.

The man before them—Mr. Cheeverly it must be—went on as if nothing were amiss. "And which of these lovely ladies is to be the bride—ah, she must indeed be the blushing maiden here. But you must not be shy with us. We are to be neighbors. Cynthia's mother told us of your coming nuptials, Staines, but what is this that you marry at Westerley? It must be that the village chapel is too small for your invitation list, eh?"

His smile widened, and he obviously intended his remark as a jest, but Eleanor found herself clenching her back teeth against such forced, awkward humor. Mr. Cheeverly had to be an utter block not to see the daggers in Lord Staines's eyes, not to notice his own wife's nervousness. But he greeted everyone in turn, happy and convivial, and Eleanor could only think that he was a rather frightening clergyman. She could just imagine him coming cheerfully to a deathbed, offering platitudes and good wishes, insensitive to the distress of others.

Lord Staines gave Mr. Cheeverly back some vague answers, exerted his skills and got them out of the building with a muttered excuse of not keeping the coach horses waiting.

But on the drive back to Westerley, Eleanor noted how silent Lord Staines was. And she wondered just what stood between him and Cynthia Cheeverly?

"You call this hall decked? Decked with what? A scrub of pine and a branch of holly? Bah! I want some proper greenery, as my poor Amanda used to have. Ivy and holly, and branches of bay as well. And that sweet smelling stuff—what it is—rosemary. Rosemary for remembrance, ain't it?"

Eleanor heard the booming voice echo up the stairs. She paused at the turn of the stair, one hand still on the carved oak balustrade. She could not mistake that voice even though she had only heard it once and it had been far softer. But what was the dying Earl doing downstairs?

She had come down early for breakfast, unable to bear her room an instant longer. Dinner last night had been a strain for her, although to judge from the chatter about the shopping expedition no one else had noticed. However, she had been too aware of the tightness around Lord Staines's mouth and of how he would at times fall silent, a distant look clouding his blue eyes. And she could do nothing for him.

She spent most of the night staring at the canopy of her bed, thinking of the day, picking it apart as if it were embroidery mis-stitched. She could not doubt that Cynthia must be the lady that he had honestly loved, but that love had gone awry. Now he simply wanted a wife. A complacent, sensible, undemanding wife. Eleanor hated that she had been cast in that role.

"*. . . to marry a gentleman who loves elsewhere. That is always disaster.*" All night, Lady Terrance's words had echoed in Eleanor's mind.

A sensible girl would turn away from this marriage. Now. Before it was too late.

But Eleanor feared it already was too late, for she found herself unable to even think of breaking this off. She could not be the cause of more pain for him, not even a mere bruising to his pride.

The voice—a deeper, more aged version of Lord Staines's own—drew Eleanor's attention back to the moment. "Take 'em down, damn you! All of 'em. I want this house decked in fresh, proper garlands! There is less than

We'd Like to Invite You to Subscribe to Zebra's Regency Romance Book Club and Give You a Gift of 4 Free Books as Your Introduction! (Worth $19.96!)

If you're a Regency lover, imagine the joy of getting 4 FREE Zebra Regency Romances and then the chance to have these lovely stories delivered to your home each month at the lowest prices available! Well, that's our offer to you and here's how you benefit by becoming a Zebra Home Subscription Service subscriber:

- **4 FREE** Introductory Regency Romances are delivered to your doorstep

- 4 BRAND NEW Regencies are then delivered each month (usually before they're available in bookstores)

- Subscribers save almost $4.00 every month

- Home delivery is always **FREE**

- You also receive a **FREE** monthly newsletter, *Zebra/ Pinnacle Romance News* which features author profiles, contests, subscriber benefits, book previews and more

- No risks or obligations...in other words you can cancel whenever you wish with no questions asked

Join the thousands of readers who enjoy the savings and convenience offered to Regency Romance subscribers. After your initial introductory shipment, you receive 4 brand-new Zebra Regency Romances each month to examine for 10 days. Then, if you decide to keep the books, you'll pay the preferred subscriber's price of just $4.00 per title. That's only $16.00 for all 4 books and there's never an extra charge for shipping and handling.

It's a no-lose proposition, so return the FREE BOOK CERTIFICATE today!

Check out our website at www.kensingtonbooks.com.

Say Yes to 4 Free Books!
Complete and return the order card to receive this $19.96 value, ABSOLUTELY FREE!

(If the certificate is missing below, write to:)
Zebra Home Subscription Service, Inc.,
120 Brighton Road, P.O. Box 5214, Clifton, New Jersey 07015-5214
or call TOLL-FREE 1-888-345-BOOK

FREE BOOK CERTIFICATE

YES! Please rush me 4 Zebra Regency Romances without cost or obligation. I understand that each month thereafter I will be able to preview 4 brand-new Regency Romances FREE for 10 days. Then, if I should decide to keep them, I will pay the money-saving preferred subscriber's price of just $16.00 for all 4...that's a savings of almost $4 off the publisher's price with no additional charge for shipping and handling. I may return any shipment within 10 days and owe nothing, and I may cancel this subscription at any time. My 4 FREE books will be mine to keep in any case.

Name _____

Address _____ Apt. _____

City _____ State_____ Zip _____

Telephone ( ) _____

Signature _____
(If under 18, parent or guardian must sign.)

RN119A

Terms and prices subject to change. Orders subject to acceptance by Zebra Home Subscription Service, Inc. Offer valid in U.S. only.

a fortnight to Christmas! Even less to the hunt meet, and this house looks as if a damn miser lives here."

Curiosity stirred, Eleanor started down the stairs again, her steps muffled by the carpet. She must be mistaken. This must be an uncle, or some other close relation, come to visit for the wedding and the holidays. Surely, it could not be the dying Earl. Then she turned the corner of the stairs and stopped in the middle of the final flight of stairs, astonished.

The hall looked as if a tree had fallen into it. Pine boughs lay on the floor, or hung like limp, dying branches from the walls as footmen scurried to pull them down. To Eleanor there seemed to be no reason to complain of a lack of greenery.

In the middle of the flurry, the Earl, shrunken, his hands shaking, sat in a wicker-backed wheeled chair. A green wool rug covered his lap and legs, and a purple dressing gown swallowed up his form. A footman stood behind the Earl, stone faced and alert, waiting for his orders.

Worry for the Earl's health tightened in Eleanor's chest. And, yet, what could she do? She was a guest in this house. She tried to turn away, to go back to her rooms. Only she could not. She had heard of conditions that afflicted the elderly, leaving them confused and apt to do themselves a harm. What if that were the case? She was, after all, soon to become much more than a guest here.

Pulling her shawl even closer against the morning chill, she started downstairs. "Good morning, sir. May I offer my help to look after this while you go back upstairs?"

For an instant it seemed as if surprise flickered in the Earl's eyes—and a touch of worry. And then all other emotion vanished under a daunting scowl.

He folded his trembling hands in his lap. "You're not yet Countess of Herndon, Miss. So you may put it out of your mind that you'll send me back to my rooms with a bowl of damned gruel. These decorations your idea as well?"

Now she remembered what Geoffrey had said—his father would like her better if she could not be cowed. Well, she had no wish for his approval, not if he were such an insensitive, horrid man. But she was not going to allow him to put himself into the grave, either.

She gave him back his stare and said, her voice soft, "My idea, sir, is that you should have better concern for your health. Geoffrey will not like it if you do yourself harm."

He stared at her a moment, then the deep lines around his eyes and mouth crinkled as he smiled. "Well, so he is Geoffrey to you, is he?"

Face warming, she did not know how to answer. Before she could get a word out, the Earl twisted in his chair and said to the footman behind him. "Robert, take me upstairs." He swung back, giving Eleanor an appraising stare, "Come, Miss, I have something to show you."

Eleanor hesitated. She did not want to be shown anything. Not by this unpleasant old man. But the footman— Robert—had already wheeled the Earl to the stairs, and with the aid of another burly footman, the two servants lifted the wheeled chair and started up the stairs.

Anything that moved the Earl towards his rooms seemed a good thing, so Eleanor followed, meek and obedient, even though the childish urge to stick her tongue out and makes faces at his back was almost more than she could suppress.

At the top of the stairs, the servants put the chair down again, and Robert wheeled the Earl down the hall that Eleanor recognized as leading to the Earl's room. They stopped, however, at the doors adjacent to the Earl's bedroom, and the footman ushered them into a dark and musty chamber.

It smelled of dry roses and the faintest touch of mold,

and the cold made Eleanor wish she had worn something thicker than her wool gown and Spanish shawl. After settling the Earl near the entrance, the servant moved at once to throw back the drapery. Eleanor heard the clatter of brass rings on the wooden rails, and then light bloomed from the gray, leaden sky outside.

What she saw pleased her.

Blue damask silk hung in panels on cream-painted wood walls. Deeper blue jacquard drapery framed the tall windows through which the pale December morning light shown. On a dresser, cut crystal cosmetic jars stood beside a set of silver-backed brushes. A bay window stood opposite the bed, and in that enclosure two chairs and a small round table made an intimate setting for a morning breakfast. Cozy in size, and distinctly feminine, Eleanor realized that this must have been the late Countess' room.

She wondered at once if this room would be hers after she married, and she could not stop the image of herself and Lord Staines sitting beside that bay window. Would he breakfast with her? Would he wear a brocade dressing gown? Or simply a white shirt and breeches? Or perhaps even less? Heat flamed into her cheeks at the images of him that she had conjured. He really would look quite devastating with his hair tousled, and his shirt open and after a night spent. . . .

She turned away, trying to distract herself with the reality before her of an empty, unused room that was no place for her.

Over the fireplace hung a portrait of the late Countess. Her eldest son did not look much like her, for she was a dark beauty, with haughty cheekbones and dainty features, and sharp, clear light-brown eyes. She carried herself like a queen and looked as if she would have been more than a match for the Earl.

"Leave us," the Earl ordered, gesturing to the footman to go. He did so, bowing himself out.

Positioned under the portrait and before the unlit fire-place, the Earl settled himself in his chair, the wicker creaking under his slight form. The sensation of being back before her old governess and about to be quizzed on a particularly difficult subject swept over Eleanor, making the back of her neck tingle and her stomach flutter. What did he want from her?

Frowning, the Earl gestured to the portrait and then said, his voice gruff, "That was my wife. Amanda. Never met anyone to match her. Not her beauty. Not her spirit. She could ride anything. Shoot like a trooper. Dance 'til dawn and then drive to London for a breakfast of ices at Gunter's."

He paused, seeming to sink in on himself, as if memories or pain consumed him. Concern for him overrode Eleanor's dislike of him, and she came forward. He really ought not tax himself in this fashion. Oh, how could she coax him to the comfort of his own rooms?

Before she reached his side, he roused. His glance—sharp and assessing—stopped her and put that nervous flutter back in her stomach. The man was worse than his son at that.

"You hunt?" he demanded.

"Hunt?" she echoed, feeling remarkably stupid.

"Hunt. Ride to hounds? Follow the chase? Dash after Charles Renauld? My wife knew how to lead the field. In fact, she started the tradition of the hunt meeting here at Christmas time."

Eleanor stiffened. She understood him at last. He intended to hold her to the standards of his late wife. She glanced at the beauty in the portrait. Well, she could not compete with that—not in beauty, or skills, or anything. So she had best be honest. She glanced at the Earl again, struggling to phrase her words diplomatically.

"Well, do you, or don't you? It is not a difficult question, Miss!"

Anger warmed her veins and she flashed back an answer. "I do not. It is a barbaric sport. And if I had my way it would be banned."

His eyes narrowed. "Squeamish, are you? Ha! You modern girls. Brought up with too much feeling and sentiment."

Heat washed Eleanor's face. "I see no fault in disapproving of a such an unequal contest. And I am not squeamish. If I were, I would faint to see that you have so little regard for your own health."

He glared at her. "Pack of nonsense. Foxes must be hunted, and my well-being is my own concern."

"No, it is also your son's concern, and he is mine. And why must foxes be hunted? Because they eat a few chickens? For that we must cause them so much fear and pain, and turn their homes into nightmares and orphan their kits?"

"Rubbish. They're foxes. You cannot pretend they feel as we do. They're animals. Vermin."

She thought of how it did feel to be trapped in a room, too many bodies pressed close, too many avid eyes on her, too many sharp tongues seeking to wound with even sharper words.

"Fear is something all creatures understand, my lord."

The Earl's eyes narrowed. He opened his mouth to tell her again what utter rot such naive sentiments were, but a softening in her eyes stopped him. Good God, the girl meant it. He shifted in his chair, and his movement caused the rug to slip from his lap. She came to him at once, picking up the rug, smoothing it into place, her touch firm and with none of the usual reluctance in the young to touch an aged, sick man.

The difference between her and that other one his son had brought to him struck him at once. What was her name? Clorinda? Christina? No, Cynthia. That was it. A

pale girl with moonlight hair, and about as much sub-
stance in her.

This one still could not hold a candle to Amanda. But
she had not run from him. And she had good hands. Elegant hands. Strong hands. He wanted his son married. He
wanted the boy married soon. But, as of late, he had begun
to wonder if he was doing wrong to push the lad into it.
He'd had a dream last night of Amanda, of her unhappy,
and superstition ran deep enough in him to make him
wonder if it had been a message from her for him to stop
pushing.

But that was rubbish as well. Was it not?

"Sit down," he ordered.

That mulish look came back to her mouth, but she
glanced around and then sat on the edge of the chair nearest him, her back straight, obedient as any simpering miss
ought to be. She irritated him by acting so meek, and he
fought the urge to be savage enough to drive her from the
room in tears.

He honestly did want his son married, after all. But was
she right for the lad?

Straightening, he turned his chair. His shaking hands
made it difficult, but when she started to rise to help him,
he waved her away.

When he could see Amanda's portrait, he relaxed back
in that damn chair.

"D'you know how she died?" he asked, determined to
find out if this Glover girl would do for his son, or if he
ought to fix Geoffrey with another of Edward's girls.

She said nothing, only shook her head, her eyes enormous and dark in that small, oval face of hers. She looked
a touch like a fox herself, with a hint of red in that sleek
brown hair, and those wide brown eyes that stared at him
as if she were a hunted creature.

He paused a moment, making her wait, and then he
said, "She went out hunting with me in an utter downpour.

Came home soaked and laughing about it. The fever came on that night. She wouldn't hear of the doctor being called. I summoned Ibbottson anyway. She died within the week. Influenza. Nothing Ibbottson could do for her. Nor I. Geoffrey was ten at the time, Andrew eight, and Patrick wasn't old enough to understand why his mother had to go to heaven without him."

He scowled. The place in his heart that Amanda had filled still ached, still lay empty and barren. He no longer wanted to cut short his own days, as he had once, trying every reckless thing he could. But he blamed those hard years for the foundation of this shaking palsy and every other ailment that now plagued him. Well, at least he'd had the boys to bring him back from his despair. And now he still had one task in life—to see Amanda's sons settled and happy, as she had asked. And, by God, he would do just that. Whether the lads liked it or not, he would.

Throwing off the memories, he looked up again to glare at this slip of a girl, this timid creature who Geoffrey had brought home. Lord, why could the boy not take a headstrong beauty to wife?

She watched him from those huge eyes, and he waited, ready to snap at her for showing him any pity. He hated those mawkish misses who cried over every damn thing. But she only sat still, listening, attentive, understanding in her eyes.

Her silence, and the innocent vulnerability in her eyes, stirred an urge deep inside him not to dig at her any more. And that gave an opening for his conscience to whisper to him.

Tell her the truth, damn you. Let her make her own choices while she can.

Only where would that leave Geoffrey?

He had seen his son cut up terrible over that other silly girl, and then abandon himself to more vice than was good for anyone. The lad needed a wife. Needed someone who could love him. And he needed it before he damaged himself in ways that could not be repaired. The Earl knew too much about that from his own past mistakes.

Damn, but he was getting maudlin himself. However, he also knew that Amanda would not have approved his plan, and this room had brought that fully to uneasy awareness.

He glanced at Amanda's portrait. And then he turned back to the girl, determined to ask her straight out what she thought of this match, and what did she feel.

Before he could even wet his dry lips, a knock on the door interrupted, and then Geoffrey strode into the room.

Ten

For an instant an awkward silence held the room. Eleanor froze still. The Earl scowled. And Geoffrey stood in the doorway, looking almost as fierce as his father.

Glancing at his father, Geoff tried to keep his exasperation in check. Devil take it, but did the man wish to be buried with a Christmas service? He had heard from a servant of the Earl's demand to come downstairs in a Bath chair with wheels upon it. And then he had heard that the Earl was ensconced in the countess' rooms with Eleanor.

For a brief moment, the thought teased Geoff that the Earl had been play acting the whole bloody time, pretending to be deathly ill to gain his own way in this matter of his heir's marriage. After all, Simon Arthur Westerley, Earl of Herndon, Viscount Wey and Baron Staines had lived for sixty-two years, burying one wife, raising three sons, ruling his domain, and manipulating others for most of that time. Poor Cynthia had utterly dreaded the Earl, and with reason, for he had made her cry upon more than one occasion.

But Geoff dismissed such a notion. Ibbottson, not his father, had written him about the Earl's limited time upon this earth. Besides, it would be like the Earl, even while dying, to still wish to manage the world around him.

Still, the suspicion that something was afoot returned

to tease Geoff as he studied his father's ruddy face, and his suspicions leaked into his voice, coming out in a clipped tone. "Good morning, Father. Eleanor. Do I intrude?"

Eleanor rose at once and went to the Earl's side and placed a protective hand on his shoulder. "Good morning. Your father and I were just getting better acquainted."

Irritation nibbled at Geoff's already sore temper. Devil take it, did she think his father needed protection? He could almost laugh, if it did not chafe so much that she had leapt so readily to take his father's side.

The Earl reached up and covered Eleanor's hand with his own, smiling, almost as if he had won a small victory. And then he said, his voice quavering slightly, "She's no ring yet. Thought you were to see to that."

Guilty enough to grow warm under his collar and cravat, Geoff glanced at Eleanor to see her reaction. She looked away, embarrassment staining her cheeks. Oh, Lord, she did care about a ring. Well, of course she would. But he had not been thinking of it, or of her, but only of his own misery. Well, that would end. He strode to the bedside to tug the bell-pull, summoning a servant.

Bellows, the butler, answered quickly enough that Geoff suspected he had been standing at the ready. The staff must be buzzing with the news that the Earl had come downstairs, and Bellows must have decided that a possible confrontation between father and son dictated the need for him to respond in person to this delicate situation.

"Bellows, please see that my father is made comfortable in his rooms again."

"So I'm to be ordered about in my own house?" the Earl demanded, sounding more a petulant child than a nobleman.

Geoff turned to him. Eleanor still stood beside the Earl, her hand on his shoulder, her eyes worried. For her sake, Geoff cut off the curt answer he had ready. Instead, he asked, his tone silky, "You feel well enough then to go about easily, do you?"

Hesitation flickered in the Earl's eyes. He glanced up to Eleanor, then slumped in his chair, suddenly looking aged and tired again. "Old men don't feel well—ever. Nothing but aches, in bed or out of it. Oh, take me back to my rooms, Bellows. The young have no use for me."

Eleanor's lips parted as if she would protest, but Geoff stepped forward to catch her hand. "Bellows, please also bring the family jewels from the vault to the library. Miss Eleanor is going to choose a ring."

He smiled at her, and she stared up at him, her eyes utterly innocent and wide, and he knew then that he would have to do more to protect her from his father's meddling. She was not up to dealing with the likes of the Earl. It would not be an arduous task, for if Ibbottson was to be believed, there was not that much longer that he would have to deal with his father.

That thought chilled him.

After seeing the Earl escorted out, Geoff offered his arm to his bride-to-be and led her from his late mother's room and down the stairs. He did not wish to talk, and, thankfully, she did not either.

He ushered her into the library, and then went to poke at the already blazing fire.

Eleanor went at once to stand beside the window and stare outside. A light snow had fallen, crisping the world as if God had sprinkled powdered sugar across the bare trees and the frozen ground. Not enough to form even a good snowball, but enough to make the ground dangerous. She hoped it stayed icy. With the ground slick and hard, there would be no fox hunting.

The door opened softly behind her, and Bellows came in, a black, leather-covered box in his hands. He put the box down upon a round rosewood table that stood near the fire, beside the tall-backed tapestry chairs and then gave a small bow.

Geoff thanked the butler, waited for the man to leave, and then told Eleanor to come and choose a ring.

She came to his side, slowly, wishing he would pick something for her. Would he never give her anything?

Geoff open the lid, and then pulled out two drawers from the front. "Which would you like—diamond, emerald, ruby, sapphire?"

Staring at the dazzling array of stones, Eleanor's breath caught in her chest. These shimmering colors drew a greed from her that she had never known to exist, and she felt as if she were a child again being offered a tray of sugared fruits at Christmas. She wanted to take more than one.

The jewels lay against black velvet: square green emeralds in a necklace, the glowing round diamonds of a brooch, the circular rubies that glinted like red eyes, and dazzling sapphires that faded when compared with his eyes. Rings, bracelets, pendants. Jewels enough to make even her dazzling to the eye.

"The tradition in our family is for the bride to have a diamond ring. There's some ancient Italian story in the family about diamonds being formed from the fires of love. I have no idea where the tale came from, and it does not seem to have much to do with us. However, anything less than a precious stone and some might whisper that I do not value you."

An odd tightness gathered around Eleanor's chest.

A precious stone, or others would think he did not consider her precious? They would think the truth. But she could not say that to him.

Instead, she frowned and said, quite honestly, "It is a pity my eyes are not blue or green, for then I could simply choose something to match."

She heard the rustle of his coat and then his scent—all warm and male—wafted closer. He caught her chin between his thumb and forefinger, turning her head, lifting her face to him. And she let him, amazed that he would touch her so, not daring even to breathe for fear she might lose that strong, vibrant contact.

"It isn't a pity," he said, his voice drifting to a rumble that vibrated in her chest. "Your eyes flash gold at times, and to match that would take the finest topaz. Only people would take it wrong if you wore something so trumpery."

The fraction of a smile lifted the corner of his mouth, and then his thumb caressed the skin just under her lower lip in the merest graze. Her skin quivered from his touch, and her pulse leapt to a wild, erratic tempo.

She fought to remember that worldly, practiced gentlemen such as he thought nothing of such a gesture.

Using the excuse of the gems to consider, she turned away, pulling back from him. And from the corner of her eye she glimpsed him frown and fold his hands behind his back.

"Choose something, Eleanor. And you do not even have to use your card to get what you want now," Geoff said, quite deliberately using her Christian name, half-hoping to provoke her into an argument. But she would not argue with him. No. She was a lady. Well bred. Refined. Better than he deserved.

Tensing his jaw until his teeth hurt, he watched her. She stood with her head bent over the jewels. Her tea-dark hair had been put up, but stray wisps had come loose to caress the back of her elegant white neck. The perverse desire rose to touch his lips to where those sable strands lay, to stroke his fingers across that skin which looked so soft.

He looked away, angry with himself. It was only a reaction to seeing Cynthia. He was just trying to obliterate her with sensations. With Eleanor. As he had done in London with any woman he could buy. It was so unfair to Eleanor to think of using her in that way. And he despised himself all the more that, even though he knew it to be wrong, he still wanted her that way. He longed for her softness. He ached for her to touch him with understanding and patience, and for her to champion him as she had his father.

But their bargain allowed no such dealings between them. They had an arrangement. Or they would if she ever thought to name what she wanted from him.

Her voice, soft as a kitten's, pulled his attention back. "This one, please."

He glanced at the ring she indicated. A small sapphire stone, pear cut, glinting with violet depths and hints of rare green fire. She had good taste in stones, he thought, approving, and half-wishing that she was the sort of woman he could buy with such gems.

Plucking the ring from its black velvet nest, he took her hand. Her cold fingers trembled under his touch. His stomach knotted. Lord, he must frighten her terribly.

He watched the pulse flutter rapidly in her throat as he slipped the ring onto her finger. In just a short number of days he would do that as the vicar intoned, "With this ring, I thee wed." Cold flooded his own hands from his fingertips to his wrists.

And then the ring stuck tight before it even passed over her knuckle. He pushed, but there was no moving it further, and so he took it off again.

Slipping the ring into his waistcoat pocket, he gave her a weak smile. Something meant to console her, and himself. "I shall have it resized in Guildford."

"Thank you," she said. She stood there a moment more, glancing about her, then she dropped a meek curtsy and fled from him. No, not fled, merely walked briskly, her back straight, to the door, and let herself out. No scene. No tears. Thank God, not as Cynthia had fled from his kisses and touches in the garden when he had tried to make love to her.

He heard the door shut behind Eleanor. Then he covered his eyes with his hand and pressed his temples to stop the pounding. And he tried to obliterate the feeling that it was a bad omen that the ring she chose did not fit. A very bad omen indeed.

Over the next few days, Geoff found no time to take Eleanor's ring into Guildford. There was a house to decorate, and redecorate, and add yet more pine and seasonal cheer to please the Earl. Dinners had to be arranged and attended, so that neighbors could meet the future Countess, and so that Rushton and his family could be kept well-entertained. Tenants had to be visited, and the estate managed. It also seemed as if one or the other of the Glover girls—never Eleanor—always had some task for him which involved their sister, and that one of his brothers had an opposite responsibility for his attention. Their tugging at him irritated, but he knew his duty as a host, and so he did his best to please them all.

Except when it came to spending any time with Eleanor.

Her, he avoided. And he kept himself too busy to even think of her, except in his bed at night, and in the early morn, when he lay upon his sheets, wakeful and restless and hating himself for what he was going to do to her. He was gentleman enough, he knew, that he would go through with this marriage. They had an agreement, after all. But he very much feared that he was also devil enough to then use her body to find forgetfulness as he had used the women in London.

Those women he had paid—or they had used him in turn. But Eleanor, wide-eyed, innocent Eleanor, knew nothing of how a man could use a woman to slake his desires, or of a man's need for mindless passion in tangled arms and sweated bodies, or how a man's lust could over-power all sense and thought and will.

He did not want to be the man who sullied Eleanor by teaching her any of those things. So, he would have to find it in him to be a decent husband. To respect her and give her no cause for complaint. And, on their wedding night, he would treat her with the delicacy and restraint she deserved. By his honor he would.

And so he fought those dangerous urges that had begun to haunt his dreams of how he longed to pillow his head upon her breast. How her hands might smooth his hair, and would feel upon his skin. He kept himself always doing something so that he would not notice her shy, in-triguing smile. He tried to ignore her melodic voice. And he forced himself not to watch her slim, petite figure as she moved about the house.

But his mood darkened each day, and he finally de-cided, as he rode back from meeting the master of the Ashford Hunt to talk about the forthcoming meet, that all his unrest was really due to that damnable card she still held.

What did she want from him? From this marriage? He could not even guess what it might be, and so her possible demands began to assume larger and larger dimensions in his mind. She had admired the gems, but had only asked for one ring—nothing else, even though the rest would be hers by her rights as the next countess. So what else might she want? Children? No, that was a given. A house? She seemed to enjoy Westerley, so why would she want more?

And then it struck him. His hand tightened on the reins and Donegal stopped, tossing his head at the sudden check.

Would she want to take a lover?

He gave a rude snort at such an absurd notion. Drop-ping the reins, he legged Donegal forward. A lover! And, yet, why not wish for someone who could give her the one thing that he could not—a man who could give her his heart? Perhaps it would not even be a man to share her bed, but one of those insufferable fops who wrote damnable poetry, sent flowers, and adored paying court to titled ladies?

Donegal shied again under Geoff's tight hand and he had to force himself to relax his stiff, gloved fingers.

Devil take it, but she couldn't want that. Could she?

With a scowl, he rode up the drive to Westerley, the gravel crunching under Donegal's hooves. Donegal's warmth seeped into Geoff's legs, but the rest of him felt as if he were made of ice. The wind whipped the capes on his greatcoat up to slap his face, tugged at his hat, and sent the bite of sleet onto his cheeks. He ignored it all.

She would not ask for a lover. No. She most likely wanted some silly thing.

Still, he decided as he swung from the saddle in the stable yard, he was damn well going to ask for that card. Now. Before another day went past. So he could stop fretting about it and they could settle into a bearable arrangement.

"We forgot something," Emma said, coming into the drawing room her face flushed and her curls in charming disarray.

Eleanor glanced up. She had been sitting with Elizabeth, working on a pair of embroidered slippers that were to be a joint present to their father. Evelyn's roses on the top looked more like pink blotches, however, and Eleanor and Elizabeth were trying to figure out something that might be done with them to make them more presentable. No matter how they looked, their father would be kind and smile, but Eleanor did so hope he would actually be pleased when he wore them.

Emma came in and sank down upon the couch opposite her sisters. She had pine needles upon her sleeves, and the sharp scene of pine and rosemary clung to her. She and Evelyn had taken it upon themselves to finish up the last rooms that were to be decorated this week, dragooning Andrew and Patrick Westerley into offering their reluctant aid.

Lady Rushton had smiled upon such schemes—it kept the younger girls from mischief, and she had confessed a hope to Eleanor that perhaps another Westerley son might find a Glover girl quite charming. However, Eleanor had seen how Patrick and Emma could not seem to be in a room together without some clash between them. And Evelyn was far too young to fix her affections upon any man.

"What did we forget?" Elizabeth said, setting aside the slippers into the embroidery basket.

"We have forgotten the mistletoe," Emma said. She pushed back a curl that had fallen forward.

Eleanor smiled. The house already could almost pass for a forest for all the red-berried holly and pine boughs and bay branches that wrapped around banisters and hung from mantels and graced the tops of picture frames and doorways.

"I do not think anyone will notice if it is missing," she said.

Emma turned an astonished stare on her. "Not notice? But of course everyone will note if there is no kissing bough!"

"She is right," Elizabeth said.

"Yes, I am," Emma added. "So would you be a dear, Eleanor, and go fetch some?"

Eleanor stared at her sister a moment, and the gave a small laugh. "You are jesting? It looks apt to snow again, and it will be dark in an hour or so, and. . . ."

"And really, Ellie. This is supposed to be the giving season, and I am only asking for this one small favor."

"But could not one of the Mr. Westerleys. . . ."

"Patrick and Andrew are helping Evelyn finish with the dining room—it is the last, you know. Lord Staines has gone out. Father is napping in the library with a book over his face. Mother is writing a letter, and Elizabeth. . . ."

"I must finish these slippers," Elizabeth said, picking one up and studying the embroidery closely.

Eleanor frowned. She enjoyed making herself useful, but she did not like this feeling of being pushed.

"Please, Ellie. Please," Emma added, her voice wistful. "You know you do not really mind, and the servants are all ever so busy just now, but I hear there is a fine crop of mistletoe not far from the stables, and. . . ."

"Oh, very well," Eleanor said, and rose with a sigh. She frowned again as a conspiratorial look passed between Emma and Elizabeth, but she could only give an inward shrug. In truth, while the day was growing dark, it would be nice to get a breath of fresh air. And she would not mind a stretch of her legs. Time, of late, had seemed to drag, for she was all too aware that Lord Staines had been avoiding her.

She must learn not to mind that. He would expect a wife to be patient and capable of amusing herself. He wanted a sensible arrangement, after all. He was simply starting off as he meant to continue with her, and she ought to feel pleased not to be pestered by his attentions.

And if she told herself that enough times she might begin to believe it.

So she told Emma not to fret, and went upstairs to change into her fawn traveling dress—for it was her warmest gown. She put on a lined bonnet, and her walking boots, then took up a brown cloak and gloves, and then went back to her wardrobe for a heavy velvet muff that would keep her hands warm. The muff would also do well enough to carry the mistletoe inside its cashmere lining. Then she ran down the stairs and let herself out of the house.

Stepping carefully across the icy patches, she headed for the stables. She stopped long enough to pet Schomberg, and to steal an extra handful of hay for him from another manger. And then she made for the woods behind the stables.

Ice and a light frosting of snow held the world silent. Wise animals huddled in their burrows, or kept to the shelter of the scattered pines. The beeches lay bare and stark, oddly attractive with their twisting branches reaching to the gray sky. While ancient, gnarled oak twisted up to the leaden skies like ancient priests reaching for the praise of forgotten gods.

Lifting her face to the cold air, Eleanor took a deep breath. The air seemed sharp as spring water and more intoxicating than champagne. It stung her cheeks and gave her a heady sense of freedom.

Dark clouds robbed the day of the last of its brightness, making the hour uncertain. Still, it was glorious to be out. To be alone. Lifting her face to the sky, she closed her eyes.

A spatter of icy rain made her open her eyes at once. She frowned, and could not help but think of the late Countess who had died from a chill she had contracted. Eleanor gave a deep sigh. She did not think she would ever be so lucky. No, she was horribly healthy and sturdy, despite her fragile appearance. She would live a very long time. Unloved. Alone in a house that did not really belong to her. With a man who did not really want her.

Geoffrey stepped into the house, stamped the ice and mud from his boots and then became aware of a stare fixed upon him. He glanced up to find the youngest of the Glover girls watching him, her hands behind her back as she stood beside the hall fire.

She looked as if she had been waiting for him—or someone—and her immediate words confirmed this.

"You are back at last. Eleanor went out to fetch some mistletoe, and Elizabeth and Emma have just begun to worry for she has been gone for ever so long."

"How long?" he asked, frowning.

Before he could answer, Patrick came into the hall. "There you are, you minx. I thought you were to help us finish decking out the dining room. Hallo, Geoff. Come and hang some holly."

Geoffrey glanced from Evelyn to his brother. He gave a small shake of his head. "Thank you, but it seems I have another task."

Frowning, Patrick started to say something, but Geoff cut him off with by saying that he would not be long.

He gave one more glance to the young Evelyn. He had no idea why she wanted him to go after her sister, but it suited his purpose quite well to do so. With a bow, he excused himself, leaving his brother to deal with this Glover. He had one of his own to find so that he could at last discover just what she wanted from this marriage of theirs.

Eleanor wandered in the woods, distracted by their beauty. A squirrel chattered at her, scolding her from the bare branches of an apple tree. She had smiled up at it, and then followed it as it flitted from branch to branch.

Rabbit tracks then caught her eye, and led her to a burrow, but no one seemed at home. She had seen a fox as well, poised on the raw, cold ground, one paw lifted, its red fur glowing with life and vitality, its whiskers twitching as it scented the wind. But she had turned away, unable to bear the thought that such a beautiful creature would soon find itself hunted by baying hounds and thundering horses.

Hurrying now, her toes growing cold and drafts of icy air slipping up her skirts to chill her legs, she moved between the patches of snow, wondering if it would snow again soon. How lovely that would be. It might make hunting impossible. It might also delay the wedding. And the insidious wish crawled loose in her that if it did, perhaps it would give Lord Staines time to fall in love with her.

But he would not. And she ought not to indulge such dangerous dreams. She might start to depend on them too much. Better to have others depending upon her. Which, she reminded herself, Emma was just now, and if she did not hurry she would have to disappoint someone she loved. She never, ever wanted to do that.

Eleanor's tracks dotted the snow, then disappeared on bare ground, but gave him trail enough to follow. He had hunted this land as a boy, and he knew how to stalk his quarry. With his hat pulled low against the cold, his hands dug into his pockets, he followed her, alternately wondering if Eleanor's sister was right to worry, and a little cross with Eleanor for going out on such a raw day. The light was fading fast and the clouds would make a cold, moonless night.

Just as he began to think that he ought to return to the house and send out every servant to search for her, he rounded a turn in the path she had taken, and there she was.

She stood in a clearing, under an ancient oak—the tree that he and Andrew and Patrick had played under a dozen or more years ago. This clearing, now frosted and barren, had once been their Robin Hood hideaway, their castle, their fort, the seat of all their childish dreams. Now it was just a patch of bare ground and an ancient and twisting oak, its branches made heavy by age and climbing vines.

She looked like some forest creature herself, clad in a brown cape so that she almost blended into the barren trees and the winter-stark ground.

Standing with her back to him, she had not seen him. She had tilted her head so far back that her bonnet had fallen off to hang down her back, kept there by only by its brown ribbons.

Then she jumped lightly up, her hand snatching at a patch of pale green vine that hung from the oak.

She jumped again, her fingers a foot away still from the branch she tried to catch.

Without waiting for her third attempt, he came forward, his boots crunching on the dead leaves and the ice that made for slippery footing. "You need a ladder—or someone with a longer reach."

She turned as he spoke, a rush of color on her cheeks. Foolish to think it could be a flush of pleasure at seeing him. The cold and her jumping around like that had brought the warmth to her face. Her seal brown hair had started to come loose from the cream ribbon that held it in place, and he almost reached out to brush one straying strand back from her forehead.

"I . . . I came out to fetch some . . . some greenery. For Emma," she said in a rush.

He raised his eyebrows at that hasty explanation. So, it was not the cold that had stained her cheeks. She seemed embarrassed. But over what?

He glanced up at the clump of soft green that dangled above her reach, its white, waxy berries now visible to him. A smile edged his mouth as he realized why she blushed.

"Greenery? A general sort of greenery, or did you have something specific in mind?" he asked, unable to resist teasing. She deserved some sort of punishment for worrying him by going out on her own. She did not know the area and might easily have gotten lost.

Her face reddened even more, but her chin shot up. "Mistletoe, actually. Emma swears we cannot have a proper Christmas without it. She sent me out to find some."

She said it as if daring him to even suggest that it had been her idea to search for a kissing bough. And he knew then that she deserved far more punishment than a mere teasing.

A smile lifted the corner of his mouth and warmed his blue eyes, and Eleanor wished she could turn to wood and grow roots. He looked as if were humoring her. As if he believed that she had made up the story that Emma had sent her out, as if she was the one who wished for a kissing bough. Drat Emma!

He pulled off one glove and reached up, stretching only a little to easily pluck down the clump of mistletoe that twined around the oak in its ancient mating of vine to tree. Then he offered it to her—only when he put it into her hand, he did not let go of it, but stared down at her, an odd light in his eyes.

"The old way is that a man should pluck a berry when he kisses a girl under a kissing bough. And when the berry is gone, there should be no more kissing."

Fascinated by the sparkling light in his eyes which shone like sunlight off a lake, she stared up at him, her lips parted and dry, and her heart thudding.

She watched his long, deft fingers pluck a berry from the clump of mistletoe that lay in her hands. He rolled the white berry between those elegant fingers and his thumb.

"We ought to keep the old customs alive, don't you think?" he said, and then he swept off his hat with his other hand, and lowered his mouth to hers.

Eleven

Before she could move, his lips touched hers, swift and sure. The soft brush of his mouth sparked a tingling heat inside her that spread from lips to face and then sank deeper, under her skin, through her heart, into her soul. Her eyes fluttered closed and the world narrowed to the taste of him, the touch of him, the scent of him which stirred her senses and whirled her mind.

And then his lips left hers. His breath whispered across her cheek, and cold slapped into its place as he pulled away.

She stood utterly still a moment, her lips parted as if the words to beg him to kiss her again would tumble out on their own. Blinking open her eyes, she looked up at him, trembling desire still quivering inside her, startling her for its unfamiliar intensity.

He stared down at her, and some fleeting emotion flashed in his blue eyes before all else fled, leaving his eyes as cold as an iced lake. Then he lay the berry he had plucked into her hands, settling it next to the mistletoe bough, and he asked, his tone flat and indifferent, "Shall we go back now?"

A lump tightened in her throat and disappointment settled inside her even colder than the winter's day. *Fool. Fool. Little fool!*

The secret she had hidden—even from herself—stood before her, stark and bare as the trees around them. What dangerous dreams she had nurtured in her deepest heart. She had thought that when they kissed, it would change him. She had no beauty, no great charm, but she had thought her love could touch him.

She had been wrong.

Now, she looked into his eyes and saw what it really meant to make an arranged marriage. He would kiss her dutifully. He would touch her only to fulfill their bargain and get a child—or two, or three, or however many he wanted. And when he had all the progeny he required, he—and she as well—would satisfy their desires elsewhere.

It would all be terribly civilized.

It would all be chillingly kind.

It would all be quite acceptable if she did not love him and long for his love in return.

Too late, she saw the disaster Lady Terrance had spoken of. Arranged marriages had no room for hearts and passion. Only for duty and indifference.

It was all too clear. It was all too late.

That kiss had not changed him—it had changed her. It had sparked a fire that had illuminated the truth. She loved him. Loved him more than was wise. Loved him more than he wanted. And she would love him even if he never loved her in return.

Still, her mind balked at the reality of her choices now. Desperation wrapped around her chest as she tried to think of some other option. But she had none.

If she rejected this bargain now, she would never have his touch upon her again. They would part and that would be an end. And she could not bear that. The kisses last only as long as the berry lasts, he had said. And then he gave her that berry back, as if he could not wait for it to be gone. But she wanted it to last—she ached for it to last forever.

Ah, he would have been wise indeed to choose a sensible miss. Instead, he had gotten a silly dreamer who wanted too much from him. But she would not tell him of his mistake. No, she wanted him too much to tell him that.

Glancing away, she curved her fingers around the berry he had held so that she would not lose it and then she tucked the mistletoe into her muff, hiding it even as she hid her feelings. He must never know. Never. She would not have him set her aside for fear that an arranged marriage would cause her too much pain. Better pain and some love than no love at all.

Summoning her courage, she looked back and gave him her brightest smile. "Yes, please. Let us do return to a fire and something hot to drink. It is rather cold."

He frowned at her, slapped his hat back on his head, and stuffed his hands into the pockets of his greatcoat. For an instant it seemed as if he would say something, but then his frown deepened to a scowl and he turned and thrust his elbow out to her, glancing back at her as if almost daring her to accept his escort.

Smile in place, she tucked her hand into the crook of his arm.

He kept his bare hand stuffed into his coat pocket, and his step shortened for her. It was the least he could do, Geoff thought, miserable and wretched. Devil take it, but he had thought to punish her—to deepen her embarrassment at being caught under a kissing bough—by giving her a kiss that would pink her cheeks. He was well served, for his plans had turned on him.

The punishment was his. Not hers. He had thought that kiss would be like the ones with the women in London— all skill and pleasant sensation, and little else. But her innocent surrender had stirred treacherous feelings inside him, and now he was in a devil of a state.

He wanted her. He wanted her in a way that brought no honor to him, and which would horrify her. For he wanted her for his own selfish needs.

He wanted to bury himself in the giving she had offered. He wanted to banish the images of Cynthia twisting in his arms, pushing him away, revulsion on her face, tears streaming loose, having to slap him to shock him from his focused desires. He wanted Eleanor to obliterate those memories.

Devil take it, he wanted something that no woman could give. He was being unfair to Eleanor to even think of asking her for such an impossible thing. And the sooner he learned that the better for them both.

Thankfully, Westerley loomed up before them. They left the woods, the icy ground crunching and slippery underfoot. Eleanor clutched his arm to steady herself, her bonnet still loose and swinging against her back, occasionally brushing against him. He forced himself not to put his arm about her trim waist, or to pick up that damn useless bonnet and put it back on her straying curls. He could not trust himself to stop at those simple gestures.

For the life of him, he could think of nothing to say. So he said nothing. Neither did she, and he wondered what was going through her mind.

At the top of the stone steps, he strode ahead to open the door for her, and then ushered her inside. She kept her eyes downcast, and her head bowed, and he could only assume he had achieved his goal—he had embarrassed her deeply with that kiss.

Devil take himself, he thought savagely.

Inside, a passing footman glanced their way, his expression startled, but he came forward at once to take their outer garments. Geoff shed his coat, gloves and hat, then he glanced at Eleanor.

She had pulled off her bonnet and cloak, and had handed her muff to the footman. The mistletoe she held in her hands. Red stung her cheeks, and the color suited her, giving life to her features. She would never be beautiful, but with such glowing skin she took the eye in a pleasing way.

"You need a fire and something warm inside you," he said, and then turned to order tea in the library. He took the mistletoe bough from her hands and gave it to the footman with a request that it be given to Miss Emma. Then he led Eleanor into the library and saw her seated in a wing armchair beside the fire.

He stood with his hands folded behind his back, and the flames warming them. Eleanor sat still, her hands closed in her lap, her eyes downcast, saying nothing until he could no longer stand it.

"I'm sorry about . . . well, you may trust it won't happen again. Not unless you . . . damn it, Eleanor, I do not know what you want of me. Of this marriage. I only know I seem to be going about this very wrongly, and perhaps it is because we really do not suit."

She looked up, alarm in her eyes. "Oh, please. I mean, I do not think a kiss is all that much to make a fuss over." She winced and bit her lower lip. It sounded as if she thought his kisses were nothing special. "I mean, I shan't protest if you wish to kiss me."

He looked away from her, and she sank back against the cool velvet of the chair with a deep sigh.

"I am not saying any of the right things, am I? But you must forgive me that, for I am not very practiced in saying much of anything to gentlemen. I never learned to flirt, or flatter. And my dratted tongue always gets me into trouble."

His gaze came back to her, but before he could answer her, a knock sounded upon the door and two footmen entered with a tea service upon a silver tray. The servants busied themselves arranging a table, setting out the tea, bowing themselves out.

When they had gone, Eleanor asked with a small smile of truce, "Shall I pour? That, at least, I can manage tolerable well."

His shoulders seemed to relax and he at last came closer, seating himself in the wing chair that faced hers. "What do you want, Eleanor? From this marriage? From me? I came looking for you, determined to have your answer on that damn card. And I vow I am as unskilled as you in this. Oh, you may well look surprised. I know my reputation with the fair sex. But I have not dealt much with wives, or soon-to-be wives. I have avoided them. So will you not help me? Will you not give me your desire on that card now?"

"I . . . I. . . ." Oh, Lord, the words hovered on her tongue, ready to fall out. She bit down hard on her right cheek to stop them. *I am not going say it. I would frighten him—and myself. And he sounds too close already to calling off this engagement.*

Taking a deep breath, she stood. "I shall get your card at once," she said. Then she fled.

Hurrying up the stairs, she reached her room, then closed the door behind her and leaned against it, eyes shut. She took three deep breaths, then opened her eyes again and strode to the writing desk. Slowly, she opened her hand where she had clutched the mistletoe berry. It was whole still.

She put it away in the drawer, tucking it inside a folded slip of paper. It was silly of her to keep it. But hold it she would—not for future hopes, but for the one brief moment of bliss that it had given her.

Then she searched the drawer for his card.

It lay where she had left it, but she had forgotten about that black blot upon it.

What did she do now? Could she tell him she had lost

his card? Or did that sound as if it had not really mattered to her in the least? Well, she would simply have to pretend she had changed her mind. That was true enough. Only what did she write now?

She stared at the card. She could not ask him for his love. No, he could not give her that and might well feel honor-bound to withdraw from their odd agreement. But could she ask to give her love to him?

The memory of how he had pulled away from their kiss, his eyes distant, slipped into her mind at once, and the hurt sliced into her fresh, deep, and sharp. No, she could not ask for that.

She strode to the window and stared out at the cold, hard world. Ah, perhaps she should give him her blank card and have done with this. Give him up and go back to a future where she would live out her days with her parents, looking after them.

Staring out the window, she wondered how the existence that she had once planned had become so unattractive?

A flash of red on the frosted ground drew her eye. She pressed her face closer to the glass and then a second reddish-brown form streaked across the frosted field. Foxes. A pair of them at play. Or perhaps hunting. She smiled as they darted into view, sleek and small. One caught the other and the pair rolled across the icy ground, and then they were up and scampering away, back into the woods again.

The awareness that she was smiling sank in slowly, and with it came the realization that she did not have to tie her world up in giving only to him. There was so much she could do—would love to do—here at Westerley. So very much.

In an instant, she was back at the writing desk. Her pulse quickened, her stomach fluttered and the daring of her idea left her a little breathless. Taking up the quill, she dipped it in the inkwell and then scrawled three words across the card. Well, whatever he might think, she knew with that this was something she wanted.

And it was done at last.

Peace settled inside her and she knew with utter certainty that if he could not give her this, there was no place for her at Westerley.

Still, her stomach began to flutter as she went down the stairs again. Just outside the library, she forced herself to stop. To smooth stray curls. To wet dry lips. Then she entered.

He looked up at once and rose smoothly to his feet, and his grace and burnished looks dazzled her again. They would always do so, she realized. It gave her such pleasure just to look upon him.

Closing the door, she gathered her nerve, and strode across the gold and brown carpets to hand him her card. "Here. This is what I want," she said, her voice rising only a little.

Geoff took the card and one eyebrow rose as he stared at the black rectangle scratched across the middle as if she had crossed out something. Then he focused on the written words and he forgot all else.

Frowning, and irritated for no particular reason, he glanced at her. "No fox hunting? What the devil does that mean? You don't want to go fox hunting? You don't wish me to?"

She stared back at him, her chin lifted, her expression calm, and the pulse thudding fast as a galloping horse in her throat. "I am asking for no fox hunting across any of your properties. Ever. Not a hunt. Not a meet. Not a chase. Not for Christmas, or any other reason."

His frown deepened. "But you don't mind other hunting? For fish or fowl?"

Her stare faltered and she began to tug on her left forefinger with her right hand. "Well, actually, I do, a little.

But shooting a bird or catching a fish seems far less cruel than chasing after an animal until it is exhausted, and then letting it be torn to bits alive, screaming, in pain, mangled to bits, and—"

"Thank you. Your description makes the difference vividly clear." He stared at the card again, rubbed his thumb across its edge, and then looked up at her. "What was this black spot?"

Her face reddened and her stare dropped to the Turkish carpet underfoot. "That was . . ." She bit off her words and looked up again, her chin taking on a stubborn tilt. "That was nothing of importance. Our agreement was that I present you the card. I have. So will you grant me what I ask?"

He let out a frustrated sigh. "Grant you? And just how do you expect me to tell everyone in the neighborhood that there is to be no Christmas meet? Nor any other. And my father. . . ." He broke off shaking his head, then frowned again. "You know, most hunts never even glimpse a flash of a fox's tail, let alone catch one."

"Yes, but the ones that do . . ."

"Die a horrible death. Yes, you've told me. And you must, it seems, rescue every dumb animal that crosses your path." *Every one but me,* he thought, and the fact that such a notion had even occurred to him irritated him even more.

Devil take it, but what was he to do with her? He could refuse her request. That would put an end to this damn agreement. But then he would have to start the hunt anew for a bride, and he could imagine having to make a worse bargain than this. She might, after all, have asked for more impossible things.

"This is unlikely to make you popular in the district, you know," he warned, half-hoping she would back down, and quite certain she would not.

Her color rose but her stare did not waver. "I did not

ask for that, did I? And, honestly, if most hunts do not even see a fox, then all that is being given up is riding over field and fences, so why cannot people do just that?"

"Because what you call riding over field and fence without a fox to set the path is little more than a steeplechase and not at all the same."

"Well, it sounds the same. So why can you not tell the master and your father and everyone that from now on—to please me—there shall be a steeplechase? We could hold one for what used to be each hunt meet day, and the first shall be this Christmas. And I shall give the winner a . . . a silver tray. That should have more appeal than catching a mangled fox."

Geoff could only shake his head. She obviously did not know the sort of avid fox hunters he knew—men who lived for the thrill of matching their wits against a fox's cunning. Gentlemen such as the Earl, and half their neighbors around them. He could not see how this could turn out well. But he supposed they could always live in London.

"Very well," he said at last. "I shall do my best to ensure your steeple-hunt day is sufficient replacement for those who live to ride to the hounds."

Her face lit with an inner glow that almost took his breath away. For an instant he thought she would throw her arms about him as she had when he had agreed to provide a home for that wretched donkey she had rescued. But, after taking no more than a step closer to him, she stopped herself.

"Thank you. Thank you so much," she said, clasping her hands together instead of clasping him. And then she turned and left him.

He stared after her for long moments, thinking only that under his tutelage she was learning to control herself. To check her impulses. And the disappointment he felt at that thought was too sharp and too real to deny.

* * *

The bell over the door jangled as Eleanor entered the jeweler's shop in Guildford. She had asked her mother if they might make one last shopping trip before Christmas, and Lady Rushton had been only too happy to request the carriage from Lord Rushton and commandeer the escort of Andrew Westerley. Emma had joined them, and while the others were busy on the High Street, admiring a set of Delft pitchers set out for display, Eleanor had slipped away.

She wanted to find something for Lord Staines—for Geoffrey. Something to give him both as a wedding gift and a Christmas gift. And she did not want others looking over her shoulder while she chose it, for it was her guilty secret that she wanted also to buy a locket for her mistletoe berry.

But I am only keeping it for remembrance of a lovely moment, she told herself. She clung to that rationalization because it was too dismal to admit to any other reason. So, she strode forward to greet the proprietor of Findlay and Finch, jewelers.

Mr. Findlay remembered her from her last visit with Lord Staines and set out a chair for her at once, and when they were seated, inquired affably how he might be of service. He wore spectacles pushed back on his balding head, and toast crumbs from his breakfast decorated his brown waistcoat and coat.

A man with toast crumbs on his waistcoat could not be intimidating, Eleanor thought. So she opened her reticule at once and took out the folded paper, which she lay on the table between their chairs.

"There are two things, actually. I would like this put into a locket, and I wish to buy a watch chain. A gold one, please."

Mr. Findlay patted his pockets, glanced around him as

if searching for something, then chuckled and reached for the spectacles perched on his head. "Mrs. Findlay owns I would forget my own address if she had not had it engraved on my watch," he confided. After adjusting his gold-wire spectacles, he took up her folded paper and unfolded it. He frowned a moment at the white, waxy berry, then glanced up over his spectacles at her.

"You wish this in a locket?"

She nodded. "A glass locket. It . . . it is a keepsake. Can you make me something before Christmas?"

He frowned again and rubbed his chin. "It might be expensive. There is the gold to acquire and shape. And the nearest glassblower is in Croydon. But perhaps if we did it as a small bottle."

Putting down the paper and the berry, Mr. Findlay patted his pockets again, dislodging the crumbs and producing a pencil from his waistcoat. He took the berry out of its paper and set it aside, and then began to sketch on the paper. "Not too elaborate. With the clasp here at the top. And it can fasten just so to the end of the watch chain."

"No. The watch chain is to be separate," she said again.

"Ah, yes. Quite so. But a loop here at the top will attach it to whatever chain you wish." He went on sketching for her, deftly drawing in the filigree work that would go around the glass locket to hold it together.

Eleanor had the distinct impression that his steady flow of conversation was more for his own benefit, for she could not follow his talk of how he would work the gold, and etch the glass, and all the rest of it. She only smiled and nodded and wondered if she could afford this.

When Mr. Findlay paused finally, she got up her courage and asked his price.

He frowned again, and rubbed his chin, and then rose and excused himself for a moment and stepped into a back room, separated from this one by a blue, velvet curtain. Eleanor waited. Deep voices rose from the back.

Then Mr. Findlay reappeared with his partner, Mr. Finch. Thin, tidy, he dressed in formal black knee breeches and coat. He shook her hand at once and then beamed at her. Mr. Findlay stood at his side, still frowning and muttering to himself, and continually pushing his spectacles up on his head and then pulling them back down in place again.

"Dear lady," Mr. Finch said, his narrow face all gracious smiles. "You must allow the firm of Findlay and Finch to make this our humble gift to you for your upcoming nuptials. It has been the honor of Findlay and Finch to serve the past two Countesses of Herndon, and we shall hope that we may continue to be of service to the next as well. Shall we not?" he added, with a severe glance at Mr. Findlay.

Mr. Findlay stopped fussing with his spectacles. "Yes, yes, of course we shall. Long tradition between our firm and the Westerley family, after all."

Eleanor understood at once. A gift now to her, with the expectation that as Lady Herndon she would continue doing business with the shop, which would allow Findlay and Finch to brag of her patronage and ensure further business with those who would be impressed by such a noble connection. It seemed a good enough exchange to her.

She thanked the gentlemen, and then Mr. Findlay recalled that she also wanted to see watch chains. Mr. Finch bought out a selection of chains on a black velvet tray. Eleanor found it a sinful delight to make a selection without thinking of cost.

She chose a gate-linked gold chain that fit at one end to a button hole and at the other to a watch. Then, glancing at a clock in the shop, she saw that she had already been away from the others for nearly half an hour. "I must go. May I take the chain with me now?"

Mr. Findlay frowned, but Mr. Finch smoothly said,

"Please, dear lady. We shall wrap your gift and have it delivered to Westerley when all is ready. And well before Christmas morn."

Letting out a small sigh of relief, she thanked them again, and hurried from the shop.

Guildford's High Street bustled with shoppers, carriages and riders. The clop of hooves sounded on hard, half-frozen ground. Carriages rolled past, and the smell of meat pies rose from the inn opposite the jewelers.

Eleanor hurried back to the china shop, intent on searching for the rest of her party there, and if she did not see them, she would wait at The Crown, where they had left the carriage.

She glanced over her shoulder to check for traffic before crossing the street, and collided at once with another person.

Instinctively, she turned and reached out to steady the other person, and found herself staring straight into Cynthia Cheeverly's silver-gray eyes.

Twelve

Mrs. Cheeverly put up a hand to grasp her poke bonnet, a plain brown silk affair whose lack of adornment did nothing to detract from her beauty. Then she gave Eleanor a brilliant smile. The potent force of the woman's charm battered at Eleanor's dislike and distrust. The shy, smiling woman in front of her seemed so at odds with the image she would rather hold of a haughty, cold beauty who had scorned a gentleman's heart.

"Miss Glover, is it not? But you are not in Guildford alone, are you?" Mrs. Cheeverly asked, her voice timid.

Eleanor's already guilty conscience flinched, and she started to explain, "No, no, I am just going to meet my mother and . . ."

"Oh, then I must walk with you. Guildford is not London, but it is large enough that it would be thought odd of you to be seen walking alone. Is your family shopping on the High Street?" She turned, took a pace and then glanced back as if waiting for Eleanor to follow, her shy smile still in place, but with an air of assurance that Eleanor wished she owned.

Frowning, hesitant, Eleanor decided that, short of complete rudeness, she could think of no way to be rid of Mrs. Cheeverly's escort. Besides, curiosity had begun to weave a net around her. She could see why Geoffrey had fallen in love with this woman's stunning beauty—but why had she not returned that feeling?

That question kept her hovering, and Mrs. Cheeverly's expectant stare drew her lagging steps forward until, with her feelings warring, she fell into step.

They did not see Lady Rushton or any of the others on the High Street, and Eleanor said at once that she could wait for them at The Crown, the inn where they had left the coach. She started again to take her leave. But Mrs. Cheeverly would not hear of it, and shook her head as if she were a dowager matron of fifty.

"Wait on your own at an inn, where you might be accosted by anyone? No, it will not do. I see now that our meeting is more than providence. You must please allow me to take tea with you and give you my company."

The words seemed quite stern, but Mrs. Cheeverly's cheeks colored prettily, and Eleanor would feel an utter beast to say no when the woman was thinking of nothing but offering assistance. And so Eleanor found herself seated in the front parlor of The Crown, with tea before her and her bonnet and jacket set upon a chair beside her, but with her feelings still at war as to how she felt about Cynthia Cheeverly.

As the landlord's wife set out a tray of tea, cakes, and biscuits, Mrs. Cheeverly spoke of inconsequential things. She asked about the steeplechase to be held in a few days, expressed her relief that her own husband showed no interest in any sport at all, but wished for good weather for Eleanor's sake.

Finally, the landlady bobbed a curtsy, asked if there would be anything else and when the ladies declined her offer, she left, saying she would inform them the instant that Lady Rushton and the others returned.

With the landlady gone, Mrs. Cheeverly turned to Eleanor and offered her shy smile again. "There, now we may be comfortable."

"Mrs. Cheeverly, I . . ."

"No, it must be Eleanor and Cynthia between us. I am determined on that. Please do tell me more of yourself. I understand that your family comes from the Lake District?"

The questions continued until Eleanor shifted uncomfortably in the wooden chair set beside the table, and then it dawned on her that Cynthia Cheeverly was as curious about her as she was about Cynthia. She did not know what to do about such focused interest, and found only that it took a great deal of effort to deal with all these questions.

Buttering a slice of bread, Mrs. Cheeverly asked, "And how do you find Lord Staines? Is he a gentleman to your liking?"

Blushing hot, Eleanor set down her tea cup. "Mrs. Cheeverly—Cynthia, do you know, I think we would both be a good deal more easy with each other if we simply spoke our thoughts—and stopped all this wandering about what it is that we each want to know."

Cynthia put down her bread, and her stare dropped to her tea cup. She turned it once in its saucer, then looked up again. "You are right. My husband claims my meddlesome nature is my besetting sin, but it is only that I truly want to help others."

Eleanor blinked in surprise. "You think I need your help? For what?"

Looking down at her half-empty tea cup again, Cynthia said, "I shall be blunt, and speak my thoughts as you have suggested. I . . . well, I have found Lord Staines to be a . . . a man of strong passions. And I know . . . that is, I worried that he might . . . that you would be . . . well, I am concerned how such passions must affect you."

Eleanor stared at the other woman during this stuttering speech. Cynthia had kept her eyes downcast and an embarrassed flush stained her cheeks. Her hands fidgeted with her tea cup, and for the first time in her life Eleanor felt as if she were the confident one in a situation. She did not—and it was probably not to her credit—feel the least bit flustered by this delicate speech. In fact, she was still struggling to sort out exactly what it was that Cynthia so obviously feared that Eleanor might be subjected to in this marriage.

Then it occurred to her that she had noticed before that Lord Staines had a temper.

"Good God, he never struck you, did he?" Eleanor asked, her face cold at such an impossibility.

Cynthia's stared jerked up. "Strike me? Really, Miss Glover—Eleanor—those are not the passions to which I refer."

"Well, what is it, then, that you seem to think he might do? Ravish me in the rose garden, or some such thing? For pity's sake, ours is an arranged match. It's you he still loves."

She could have laughed at this suggestion that Lord Staines might be so overcome by his "passions" that he would throw himself on her. Except that laugh caught in her chest and tightened around her heart, making her words come out with a harsh bitterness she had no right to feel.

"I beg your pardon," Eleanor muttered at once. "That is too much plain speaking."

Cynthia's pale, delicate hand fluttered in the air. "Oh, no. Not at all. If anything I should beg your pardon for having brought up this subject, but I . . . well, I ought to have realized that the situation would be different in an arranged marriage. Of course it must be."

Mrs. Cheeverly sounded relieved, and that kindled a sudden, deep irritation in Eleanor. She did not want this woman's pity.

"You mean that with an arranged marriage that sort of uncomfortable passion need not worry me," she said.

Seeming to take in only her words and none of the frustration behind them, Mrs. Cheeverly smiled. "Yes, exactly. Oh, I can see now that you will be comfortable with Geoffrey in a way which I never could have been."

Eleanor found herself staring at the beautiful blonde next to her, more astonished than ever. "Is that all his love was to you—an uncomfortable passion?"

"Of course not. Love, when it is pure and noble, is the most exalted of states. It is a communion of spirit that transcends the mere physical side of our animal nature. It can make us into beings of light and happiness." She frowned suddenly and the light in her eyes dimmed. "But, to my regret, I discovered one shameful day that I could never have that with Geoffrey."

"Because of his . . . his passions?"

Ducking her head, Cynthia started turning her tea cup. "My father, God rest his soul, was in the army, and I can recall him coming home on leave when I was quite young. He was a large man, or he seemed so to me—all whiskers and gruff voice. He was like one of those fearsome giants from a fairy tale. And when he came home, he would grab me up, so that my face pressed into his wool jacket, which smelled of tobacco and mustiness and other things, and spin me around and squeeze me and I could not cry out for my face being muffled. I used to run and hide when I heard him.

"Geoffrey became like that to me. He . . . well, let us just say that his passions overcame the consideration he had shown me prior to that, and when his arms went around me . . . oh, it was just like being stifled in my father's arms, only this time I could scream."

"And did you?" Eleanor asked, fascinated, her sympathies caught up with Cynthia. How awful to feel such panic, not in a crowd, but in a man's arms.

Mrs. Cheeverly nodded and started to say more, but a knock on the door interrupted, and then Lady Rushton and the others swept in, with Andrew Westerley's arms full of packages and Emma chattering questions about what they had bought and seen.

Introductions had to be made, and the moment for any more intimate conversation passed away. Mrs. Cheeverly put on what was either a mask of self-control—or such a placid face that Eleanor started to wonder if that was not her natural inclination for dealing with everything.

The talk flowed around her, and Eleanor let herself fade into the background to deal with the thoughts swirling around her mind. A small part of her triumphed that this woman had never really loved Geoffrey, not the way he deserved to be loved with a woman's heart and body. Yet she also wanted to shake Cynthia for being such a goose as to choose comfort over passion.

Eleanor shuddered at the thought. But at least Cynthia had had the choice. Eleanor had denied herself even that by agreeing to a loveless match.

On the return trip to Westerley, her mind turned not to her own choices, however, but to Geoffrey's. And to what it must have done to him to have the woman he loved reject his embrace, his heart, his desire.

Was that something from which any man could ever recover?

"You did what!" the Earl bellowed, sitting upright in his bed, his face red and the veins at his temple pounding.

Geoff had braced himself for an unpleasant interview, but he had seen no way other than to blurt out the truth. Even from the confinement of his rooms, his father must hear about the steeplechase.

Taking an even tighter hold over his own shortening temper, Geoff tried to relax the knotting muscles in his lower back. It would serve no good if he got into a shouting match with his father over this damnable event.

"You heard me quite well, sir," he said, intentionally

forcing himself to lounge with his arm across the mantel over the fireplace. "And I wish you would calm yourself about it."

"And I wish you would explain yourself! Who do you think you are, making promises with my land? I am not yet in my grave."

"You may look to be so soon enough if you give yourself an apoplexy over this. I only did as you bade me. You wanted me to marry, and this is the price of it. But if you would just as soon I not wed, then I shall go and . . ."

"Come back here at once!"

Geoff had started to turn away, but now he paused.

The Earl fell back against his pillows and glared at his son, his blue eyes icy. "Giving me no choice in the matter, are you?"

"As much as I had."

"So, this little Glover girl is going to have you dancing to her tune?"

"Not at all. It was our agreement that she ought to get something out of this arranged match. This is what she wants."

The Earl gave a harsh snort. "A title, your name, and wealth ain't enough for her?"

A smile lifted Geoff's mouth and his mood. "No, sir. They were not. And, to own the truth, I think the better of her that she values a good number of other things over wealth, my title, and our name."

"Oh, so that's how it is? You agree with this nonsense of hers? What will you next take up to please her? Eating plants only, like some damn sheep?"

At this intended insult, Geoff's back tightened again, but he only said, "Sir, if the last countess could set a tradition of the hunt meeting here, I do not see why the next one cannot remake it. She hurts no one with this request."

"Except you. She makes you a damned laughing stock."

"If that is all it takes to do so, then it sounds a fate I

deserve. Now, I bid you to rest yourself. And unless I hear from you that you do not wish me to marry, then I will assume this plan has your blessing."

With a short bow, Geoff strode from the room. He did not mind when his father battered at him, but it stung like a whip of nettles that the Earl should so attack Eleanor. She had done nothing to deserve it. And if his father kept up this behavior, then he would have to settle her in London once they were wed. It would be ironic indeed if the event his father had so longed for—his son's marriage— served to be the wedge that drove father and son apart.

Lord, had there ever been such a Christmas?

But just now, he had a more immediate future to contrive. A hundred details awaited him. He had offered to ride over the property with Eleanor to select a suitable course, choosing the steeples or high landmarks that would be chased. Already, Bellows had written out the invitations and sent them around. Refreshments would be those traditional ones from the meet—orange biscuits, Shrewsbury cakes, cold meats, beer from the home farm brewery and sherry from the cellars. Afterwards, at the end of the day would come the tenant's Christmas ball.

And the next day came his wedding.

Geoff's mouth dried and his hands went cold.

Just as well, he thought, dragging on his gloves and shouldering into his coat and focusing on anything other than his wedding. Just as well that he had too much to do and no time to think about the loveless future that came after that blessed event.

Taking up his hat, he strode for the door. At least he could get out of the house and away from his brothers's concerned stares, which had followed him about since he had told them of the steeplechase, and away from his father's recriminations. Devil take it, but this was proving as awkward as he had warned Eleanor it would be.

He found Eleanor waiting for him in the stables. Or,

rather, not so much waiting as standing in a semicircle of grooms, with them staring intently at her chest.

Suddenly, that cut it. It was one thing to have his father attacking her character, but he would damn well not put up with servants leering at her as if she were some Covent Garden doxy. Utter fury swept into him as he strode into the stables, determined to have done with this disrespect for her.

"What the devil is going on here?"

The sound of Geoffrey's low-voiced growl startled Eleanor, and she spun around to face the stable entrance, her heart thudding, her arms instinctively closing around the soft, white animal in her arms. Too weak to struggle, the rabbit burrowed its head under her arm, and she wished she had somewhere to hide as well.

Oh, no, he does not look as if he is going to like this.

Lord Staines stared at her from the wide double-doors that led into the stables. The capes on his greatcoat fluttered from his broad shoulders like the cape-fur of a wolf. With the light behind him, his handsome features were half-shadowed by his hat, worn at a rakish tilt. He looked like one of those perfect fashion plates in gentlemen's magazines come to life—and not at all like a man whose face would soften at the sight of a half-grown, injured rabbit.

Her stomach clenched in a sick knot of fear.

The grooms who had been gathered around her in a semicircle fell back a step and she could not blame them. She could not help taking a small step backwards herself, her boots scuffing on the brick of the center aisle as Lord Staines came towards her, glaring at the grooms. Even the horses who had leaned their heads over their loose boxes—as if they, too, had wanted to see what was toward—stirred nervously, the straw crunching pungent and sweet under their hooves.

"Please don't kill it," she begged, half-turning from Staines to shield the injured rabbit.

He paused a moment, his faced creased with confusion. He glared once more at the grooms, and then looked down at the rabbit that she clutched to her chest.

"Oh, for . . . is that what they were . . . they were staring at a rabbit?"

"Well, yes. What else?" she asked, blinking up at him.

He frowned at her, looked as if he might answer, then pressed his beautifully shaped lips together and shot another glare at the grooms, who darted quick bows in response and recalled work to do elsewhere.

As the grooms scurried away, Staines plucked the rabbit from her, holding the animal by the scruff of its neck. Even with the left front leg splinted, the creature's hind legs kicked out, strong and sharp-nailed.

"Not a bad job, though you would do better to keep him in your room. It's warmer, and no one will think to do away with him for a stew pot."

Her face relaxed and warmth stole back to her cheeks. She smoothed a hand over the animal's kicking hind-quarters to still it and to reassure herself that all would be well. "I did not want to be a bother. Tully and George and Brian were just going to help me sort out where I might keep him. I thought he might frighten the maids if I kept him in the house."

"Tully and George and Brian?" His mouth twisted down for a moment, and he glared after the departed grooms.

Oh, the . . . the devil take him, Eleanor thought. What was wrong? He was acting like a . . . well, like a jealous idiot. But he could hardly be that when he did not really care for her. It must simply be that something had roused his natural territorial instincts.

He turned back to her, a smile curving his lips, and that set her heart fluttering in a different way than it had earlier. Then he set the rabbit back in her arms. "I have the feeling that the maids shall have to get used to him, and others such as him, being around. And I wish you would stop trying not to be such a bother. That bothers me more than anything else."

After a glance around the stables, he strode to a corner near the door. He took up a small wooden crate, pulled two horse brushes out of it and replaced them with a handful of straw from the nearest stall.

"Your pardon, Donegal, but you must share your bedding," he told the gray gelding as the horse nosed first his hat and then breathed into the crate.

Rising, he brought the crate of straw to her, and held it as she settled the injured rabbit inside. The animal stuffed its face into a corner and stayed there, its breathing rapid, its brown eyes peering up from between yellow blades of straw and its white and pink ears pinned back.

Looking as frightened as Eleanor had when I came across her, Geoff thought, and the image left him feeling wretched. Of course, he'd only been worried for her. And about how the grooms seemed to be eyeing that trim figure of hers.

But now he realized that he had not done anything to put her at ease with him, to make her feel as if he would look after her. No, he had been too taken up with his own dark moods and his own feelings to spare any thought for hers. Well, they would both be better served if the next few days gave them at least a chance to feel comfortable with each other before they pledged the rest of their lives to each other. After all, he did not want a white-faced, trembling bride staring at him from the end of the wedding aisle. A lovely Christmas present that would be.

Glancing down at the rabbit, he absently stroked its ears. "Take him to the house, Eleanor. And when you come back, I promise to have the horses ready so that we can choose this course of yours."

She blushed prettily, and he had the impression that she might have reached out to hug him if she had not had a box of rabbit in her arms. But then she was gone, out the door, taking herself and her rescue away.

He looked after her a moment, then turned and shouted for Tully and George and Brian.

They covered a good deal of land in short order, riding as far east as the village of Albinger, then turning north to Nutley Heath and Horsley, and then west and south to Lostiford. The villages made a rough triangle around Westerley. Eleanor, he found, had some sensible ideas to keep the race within the view of the house and those guests who were not riding, so they settled eventually on a three-mile course that kept the course on either common land or property held by the Earl of Herndon.

Eleanor was, Geoff noted with some relief, an able horse-woman, despite her aversion to fox hunting. He had mounted her on Patrick's old bay hunter, Bonhomme, who lived up to his name in being a simple, solid sort of fellow. She did not seem to mind her large, staid mount, and he noted that she sat well on a horse, her back straight and not the least twisted by the side saddle, her hands light and not clutching at the reins for her balance. He would have to see about getting her a less sedate mount than old Bonnie.

She also seemed quite at ease with the tenants and neighbors they chanced upon. Shy, of course. He would have expected no less from her, but that quivering fear he had glimpsed in her at their engagement ball did not re-appear. It must indeed be crowds that bothered her, he decided, and not people in general. Still, he wondered if she would be able to carry off the duties of a countess—or even the responsibilities of acting as hostess for this damn steeplechase-hunt of hers.

Geoff glanced over to her, fretting, but then his face re-laxed with a smile at the picture she made. Perched on the dark, huge Bonhomme, she almost looked a child, with dark strands of hair slipping loose from her hat to dance in the breeze around her face. Only those were no childish curves set off by the close fit of her riding habit. Wind and cold had stung color into her cheeks, and she gazed about her with her eyes bright and lively with interest.

As if sensing his stare, she glanced over to him, and then offered back a smile that seemed an invitation to share her delight with the world.

Heat rose up into his face, and suddenly he had to be doing something. Doing something to get rid of the urge that had risen to grab Bonnie's reins and drag him to a halt so he might lean closer and indulge in foolishness.

"Come along, race you to the stables," he said, and with a cluck to Donegal, he loosened the reins, letting the gray surge forward into a canter.

"No fair," Eleanor cried out. Then he heard her urging the placid Bonnie forward.

He checked Donegal to give her a chance to catch him, but then the huge, dark hunter surged past with surprising speed. Leaning forward and tiny on Bonnie's back, her reins loose and flapping, Eleanor flashed back a grin at him. With an oath, Geoff dug his heels into Donegal's sides and galloped after her.

She beat him to the stables by a neck's length, and pulled up, then turned and leaned down to pat the steaming, dark gelding.

"And that is what you get for thinking this old gentleman had no spark in him," she told him.

"I haven't seen old Bonnie make a run like that in years," he said, swinging out of the saddle and tossing the reins to the nearest groom. He strode at once to Eleanor as she unhooked her leg over the pommel of the side saddle and untangled her skirts.

He reached up for her. She hesitated a moment, and then slid down into his arms.

His hands fit neatly around her trim waist, his fingers

not quite touching, but closing easily around the supple curves. The heat and smell of horse wove around them, holding off the chill. She stared up at him, her eyes enormous, her gloved hands on his shoulders, her touch light but somehow intimate.

He had meant to let go at once. To do no more than provide the courtesy of assisting her, but then Bonhomme turned and shoved his nose into Eleanor's back, rubbing his sweated ears against her and thrusting her full into Geoff's arms.

Devil take it, he thought, mouth drying and pulse accelerating. *No, devil take him.* She fell against him, all soft curves and sweet yielding, and he could only think of that kiss he had stolen under the mistletoe bough, of how her lips had tasted, of how he wanted to lose himself in her arms.

Donegal's snort and the clop of hooves on the brick stable yard pulled him back to reality, reminding him of the grooms standing about, watching. And that he was not about to risk offending his bride by presuming too much before they were wed. No, he knew the danger of that.

He put her away from him at once. "Excuse me. I must see to the horses," he said and strode at once for the stable, his skin still burning and uncomfortably aware of her stare on his back.

Eleanor continued to stare after him. She knew she should not. So dangerous to watch him. So hopeless to yearn after him. Emptiness lay inside her, like a chasm that had cracked opened. She had to accustom herself to it, that was all. What was it he had told her at the ball to give her confidence? Ah, yes, she had to learn how not to care. She really, really must.

She knew now, after her talk with Mrs. Cheeverly, that he had had good cause to help him develop his own uncaring heart.

A spark of anger flared in her. Anger at him that she

must learn this harsh lesson. But she had agreed to it by agreeing to this marriage. So she put her chin up and turned away from him. She kept her steps firm and refused to even acknowledge the ache that lay deep inside her chest. She would learn how to not let this matter to her. She had to. For she no longer could face the option of having to learn how to live without him.

The marriage settlements were signed and concluded. Geoffrey watched as the lawyer held out the paper with the terms of dower for his wife and which outlined her quarterly allowance. He found himself curiously detached, as if he were watching it happen to someone else. That did not surprise him. The settlements had been something for the family solicitors to sort through—though Lord Rushton had expressed his wishes for the financial arrangements to assure his daughter's future. And the Earl had wanted to know what property came to the family through the alliance.

It all seemed so ridiculously reasonable. Nothing of feeling in it. Nothing of passion. Nothing about a request for no fox hunting.

"What are you smiling at?"

Geoffrey glanced up at his father's scowling face. The Earl had dressed for this occasion and had come downstairs to the library, the footmen carrying him in his wheeled chair.

"Nothing, sir. Or perhaps it is just with relief to have it done. Now, if you will excuse me, I do have other duties—and a steeplechase to arrange."

The Earl glowered, but waved a dismissive hand at his son. And then one at the solicitors. "Oh, go away. Go away. Not you, Edward. You'll stay and have a glass of something with me, to toast the couple's future?"

Thirteen

Lord Rushton hesitated. "Are you certain you should?"

"Don't you start prosing on at me. I get enough of that from my sons. And if one drink kills me, then your daughter is a countess that much sooner."

Coming back to the chairs beside the marble fireplace, Lord Rushton smoothed aside the tails of his coat and seated himself in one of the leather wing chairs. "Ellie's not ready to be a countess, so I would appreciate it if you would extend yourself to live a good while longer. Ah, thank you, Bellows," he added, turning to the butler who had appeared with two glasses of port.

The last rays of the setting sun streamed into the room from under dark clouds that had gathered in the west, giving a pale, golden light to the room. A soft click of the door announced Bellows's discreet departure, leaving behind only the quiet of the mantel clock ticking, and the faint hiss and warm aroma of the pinewood fire.

Lord Rushton settled himself more easily next to the fire, then raised his glass. "To the young couple—happiness, good health, and strong children."

The Earl raised his glass as well, his hand trembling only slightly. "Aye, to grandchildren for us both at last." He drank back half the dark red wine, and then slumped in his chair, staring into the fire, his stare absent and his lined face unsmiling.

Lord Rushton gave a small chuckle. "What is it, Simon? You look as cheerful as if you had signed your own death warrant, not your son's marriage settlements."

Rousing, the Earl looked up. "But have we done good work today? I worry about this. Have ever since I met that gel of yours. Slip of a thing. Is she up to him, Edward? What if we have just settled them the devil of a future together?"

Lord Rushton's hand stopped with his glass half-raised to his mouth. His face flushed red, and then he slowly lowered his glass. "Are you implying that I'd marry one of my daughters off for no better reason than getting a ring on her finger? That I have not acted with her best interests in mind? By God, if you weren't in that chair, I'd plant you a facer that would put you in one!"

"You would, now?" The Earl slammed his glass down on a side table, and then pushed himself up from his chair until he stood on his feet, steady even if hunched by age. The rug that had lain across his lap fell aside and he raised his fists before him. "Come on, then. Have at me. See if you can!"

Lord Rushton stared at him a moment, his face incredulous. Then he gave a laugh, and said, "For pity's sake, let us not be old fools at least. Sit down. Sit down, man. You're about to become my kin, not my enemy. And you may stop glaring at me. I doubt neither your pride, nor your abilities—which is exactly why this marriage seemed such a godsend. I knew you'd have raised your sons to be decent men—despite the rumors about your eldest."

Slowly, the Earl settled himself in his chair again, giving out a deep breath as he did so and fumbling to put the green, woolen lap rug back across his legs. "Bah—rumors! I'd have been worried if Geoffrey hadn't earned himself something of a reputation. Young men need their fun—up to a point. But I thought your gel could settle him. Only here she is with these odd notions of no fox hunting, and heaven only knows what else in her head. What kind of girls are you raising to be so hen-witted?"

Lord Rushton flushed. "I am raising, I should hope, young ladies of sensibility as well as sense. Eleanor has the kindest heart of all of 'em—and she has the best mind, as well. So I should thank you not to call her hen-witted. She's a well-behaved girl, and I don't think there is anything to worry over. Which is why she seemed perfect for your Geoffrey, and why we should let these two sort it out for themselves. It is they who must come to an understanding of heart and mind. We can only tie up the legal bits of it."

With a rude snort, the Earl took up his glass of wine and stared into it. "How can any man understand a woman who don't hunt?"

"Your son don't seem to be bothered by that. And that gives me reason to have hope there . . . yes, I have hopes."

The Earl looked up sharply. "Just what do you mean? We all have hopes for 'em. My poor Amanda had hopes for 'em—and, by heavens, I'm going to see that her wish for them to be happy is fulfilled."

"Then leave off your schemes—and don't turn that innocent, aged stare on me and try to pretend you're a doddering old man who can't even dress himself. I am not here to put a spoke in the wheel of whatever game you have spinning, Simon, but I caution you that this wedding and this marriage going right depends more on your son and my daughter than on either of us. So leave them to it. I am. It's hard I know, but they have to bruise their own shins. Or do you not trust your own son's instincts in such matters?"

The Earl grumbled something into his glass. He hated to admit it, but his friend was right. And it irritated him enormously, for he could not help but remember how short a time it seemed since he had held his first-born in his arms and had ached with the desire to do anything and everything to protect that wriggling, red-faced babe.

He let out a long sigh. "Damn you. It is up to him. And that gel of yours. So let us both drink to the hope that they know their own hearts well enough before they wed, or that knot will stick tighter about their necks than that of a hangman's noose."

The morning of the steeplechase dawned bright, with billowing clouds scudding across the sky, driven fast by a cold east wind. Dark and threatening, the clouds scattered fat droplets of rain as they passed over the barren, winter fields and the green hills that lay around Westerley. Those with aches in once-broken bones predicted a downpour before this steeplechase nonsense of the new Countess-to-be even started. The more optimistic glanced to the sky, lifted a wetted finger to the wind, and thought that it might yet turn into a bright winter's day. However, all in the neighborhood agreed on one thing—sun, rain, chill wind or none, this event was not to be missed.

The food would be plentiful and free, and the drink even more so. But the larger draw was the chance to see the Earl—and possibly see him lose his famous temper over this new start of his son's bride. Everyone knew, after all, how hunting-mad the Earl and his Countess had been. Why she had even died from a chill taken while hunting. Of course, if the Earl did not appear, there was still his son to watch, and the curiosity to satisfy of how this bride of his had gotten him to agree to so foolish a thing as to replace fox hunting on his property with a mere steeple-chase. Finally, there would be the bride herself to glimpse and perhaps meet.

The gossip in the neighborhood divided sharply on her, with those who had chanced to encounter her claiming that she was a timid lady with too tender a heart, and the rest proclaiming that she obviously intended to make her husband dance to the tunes she called. In general, all agreed upon one other thing, and that was that this marriage would be as large a disaster as this mad start of hers about steeplechases.

Nothing, after all, could replace the thrill of a fox hunt in full cry across the fields, with the huntsmen's red coats flashing, the fine horses galloping past, and the hounds baying. And nothing could replace the previous Countess, with her free laugh and her easy ways and her love of sport. The young lord had gotten himself a bad bargain with this arranged match of his.

So it was that everyone came to Westerley with full expectations of entertainment in the form of watching how badly this new bride-to-be behaved, and with half those gathered hoping some argument might break out and end this marriage before it began, and the other half ready to feel sorry for Lord Staines and the wife he would be obliged to endure.

Eleanor had no awareness of the expectations that hovered around her as she stepped from the house to greet the first guests that had arrived, and to take on her role as hostess.

She had not slept well, what with worries about this day and the next, with her nerves strung too tight, and trying to rehearse in her mind a calmness that vanished as soon as she saw how many had already assembled at Westerley.

She almost turned and went back into the house.

But Andrew Westerley came out as she turned to the front doors. He offered a smile and his arm and then said as a few rain spatters darkened the shoulders of the capes to his greatcoat, "It is a excellent day for a race. The horses shall be fresh as this wind and we should see some good sport from them. Ah, Geoff is already talking to Squire

Boscomb—he is the Master of the Hunt, you know, and he is to ride in the race as head steward to see that all's fair."

She glanced to where Lord Staines stood with an older, stocky man whose legs were as bowed as if he had been born on a horse. Then she glanced back to Andrew. "Was the squire very much upset?"

"With what? Not hunting? Oh, he still takes his pack out. He holds a good deal of property south of here. And I cannot think he minds all that much. It was his idea to ride as steward. Said it would give him the best view to be in the midst of things. Personally, I think he wants to see Archie Dunleigh tossed by that red brute of a horse he bought from the Tinkers this fall. Odds are the horse shall finish the course, but not with Archie. Now, come, I shall take you about and tell you which of the riders to bet upon."

He did so, distracting her with harmless tales about the various horses and riders so that she almost forgot the quivering fear that lay just under her pretense of calm control.

Being in a crowd out-of-doors was not so bad, she found. The bite of the wind kept away the terrifying suffocation that had made London ballrooms so dreadful. And while the numbers of those gathered steadily grew until it seemed as if all the front terrace and gravel drive and even the lawn was covered with horses and carriages and milling people, still there was plenty of space to walk and no one pressed too close.

Andrew stayed with her. He introduced so many neighbors that she would never be able to sort out faces and keep the names all straight. He pointed out the best horses: Squire Boscomb's raking black gelding, which surely would have won had he entered, and a compact gray thoroughbred owned by a Mr. Josiah, which Andrew assured would finish in the top three at the least.

But while he tried to amuse her, Eleanor found her attention slipping back to Lord Staines.

He made no effort to approach her, and she tried not to mind his neglect. He was busy. He had duties and guests to greet, and he did not need her making demands upon him like a petulant child. She had asked for enough, after all, in asking for this event.

Still, a small voice whispered, the least he could have done was to come over and say good day. And for that her heart ached.

He looked so dashing, with his golden locks left uncovered by a hat, his wide shoulders displayed in a fitted brown riding coat, and his muscular legs shown off by buckskin breeches and white-topped riding boots. He had to be the most handsome man here. The others had bundled up against the wind and the possibility of rain, but not him. He seemed able to defy the whims of mere weather.

Stopping next to a lady in a sage-green riding dress, Staines paused and bent his head as the lady spoke to him. His gesture and closeness to the lady spoke of shared intimacy, and Eleanor suddenly froze. Oh, why had she not thought of this? Of course a man such as he, with his reputation, would be bound to meet other ladies he had known—and known well.

She glanced away, determined not to care. To ignore the hot churning in her stomach. To pretend indifference.

But she had to look back. She had to know what he was saying to her now.

Then the lady turned and Eleanor saw that he was talking to Mrs. Cheeverly. To his Cynthia.

Gone was the drab brown bonnet and dress of a curate's wife. Her riding habit was old, but in a classic, military style. Its severe lines suited her, offering a provocative contrast to her slender curves. A pert military shako allowed golden curls to peek out at the sides, and a green plume curled next to her face, dancing in the wind and caressing the perfection of her cheek.

Lord Staines held out his hand to her. She hesitated a

moment, looked down at his hand, then glanced up and smiled. Eleanor's stomach twisted into a hard knot and her throat tightened. She wanted to look away, but she could not. They looked too perfect together. Too utterly right. And she was not the only one to think so. For she heard the whispers.

"What a pity they did not make a match of it."

"So striking, aren't they?"

But the final blow came when a woman next to her whispered to her gentleman friend, "Ah, what beautiful children they would have had."

Eleanor turned away then, her cheeks burning. She could not blame Cynthia and Lord Staines for how ideal they looked together. It was as if they had been fashioned to go together, like perfect, matching figurines.

Oh, that stupid, stupid woman. She ought to have married Geoffrey! No, not Geoffrey, she told herself. Lord Staines. Far better to put a proper distance into this arranged marriage and to remember that it held no promise of closeness or feeling.

Ah, but she was being foolish to care. Silly to let this tear at her, like a cut from a rose thorn across her heart. It seemed that she had not yet fully learned her lesson of how to protect herself. But in that instant, however, she knew now that to survive this marriage she must build some sort of armor. She had to or she would destroy herself with this wretched longing.

Glancing up at Andrew Westerley, she saw that he, too, was staring at his brother and Mrs. Cheeverly, frowning, with worry in his eyes. *Ah, he cares for Geoffrey, too. We all do, and yet none of us can do anything.*

But there was something she could do. She could distract herself and Andrew so that they did not have to dwell upon impossible wishes.

So she asked Andrew where his brother Patrick might be, and when he said that Patrick had gone out upon an

errand, she asked if he would help her find Emma and
Elizabeth and Evelyn in this crowd.

It was better doing something. But it did not do away
completely with the ache inside, nor the awareness of how
Lord Staines still stood talking with Mrs. Cheeverly.

"What do you mean, you've lost the ring?" Geoff demanded.

He stood on the steps to the house. The steeplechase
had to begin soon. Dark clouds now piled against each
other in the west in an ominous stack, and would probably
soon loosen a bitter-cold drenching rain. On the lawn, the
riders—ten of them racing, and Squire Boscomb, along
with two grooms from Westerley to aid him as stewards—
now formed a ragged line, their horses restless and pranc-
ing and ready to run.

Geoff regarded his youngest brother with mounting irritation. Devil take it, bad enough to have to meet Cynthia
here, with her looking like the girl he had once known
and loved. At least it had given him a chance to cry friends
with her again. But now this. And here was half the county
gathered and eager for hints of scandal. He had not missed
the speculative stares following him and Eleanor this day.
How the devil much more bad luck was he to run into?

Patrick's stare fell to the stone steps. Mud from the
road to Guildford spattered his boots and buff buckskin
breeches, and his bottle-green coat hung open over a buff
waistcoat.

"How was I to know the damn thing wouldn't stay in
my pocket?" he grumbled, looking as if he were a school-
boy of thirteen and not a supposedly responsible gentleman of twenty-three.

Since he was not riding in the steeplechase, he had
accepted Geoffrey's request to go to Guildford to collect
the wedding ring this morning.

Now, Geoff's jaw tightened, and the muscles bunched in his shoulders until it felt as if the seams of his jacket must split. He ought to have had Findlay and Finch deliver the dratted ring. Only it had seemed such a simple thing to send Patrick after it.

Simple! He ought to have known better.

Hot, angry words began to pile up in his mind, but then he glanced at Eleanor.

She stood next to Andrew, remarkable in the crowd only by virtue of being a slip of thing. Dressed in a dark green riding habit, with a faint flush warming her cheeks, and her dark hair already starting to stray from a confining bandeau meant to hold them in order, she looked charming. Not pretty, but charming. And it struck him that he liked how those seal-brown strands had a mind of their own, never holding in place, but straying into wisps that caressed her cheeks and the white nape of her neck.

His anger cooled as he watched her. If he made a scene about the ring, she would know. Devil take it, everyone would. And she—as well as others—might see it as a bad omen. He knew enough of weddings to know they came wrapped in superstitions. And too many here were eagerly seeking signs of impending disaster.

Taking a deep breath, he forced his jaw to loosen and then he clapped Patrick on the shoulder. "Never mind. Just don't tell anyone. I don't want mutters of bad luck starting up. And you may get yourself back to Guildford to ask Findlay and Finch for another ring to match the fit they made of that one's size. I'm certain it will be devilishly expensive, but that's no matter."

Wary, Patrick eyed his brother. "You're not angry with me?"

Geoffrey's mouth lifted. "Don't sound so disappointed. I still plan to flay you alive if you lose this second one. Now, go and make good on this mishap by coming up with a new ring for me."

With a flash of a smile, Patrick started down the steps. He paused at the base and glanced up again. "I didn't mean to lose it, honestly I didn't. It's not as if I don't want to see you married. Andrew and I both want to see you happy. Really, we do."

Then he bolted for the stables, leaving Geoffrey staring after him, puzzled and wondering what the devil that speech had meant.

It occurred to him then that both his brothers had been acting odd of late, seeming to go out of their way to insert themselves between him and his bride-to-be. Each evening one of them had fitted himself to Eleanor's side.

Irritation with them had nibbled at him on more than one of those occasions for monopolizing her time. But he had thought that they were doing no more than going out of their way to make her feel welcome into the family. Now he wondered if other motives prompted such gallantry.

Had they been trying to manage his affairs for him?

He'd bloody wring their necks if they had. Devil take it, but could not any member of his family allow him to make his own life? Here was his father, wanting him to marry, but not wanting him to wed Eleanor. And were his brothers out to also ensure that his marriage took place? Did they all think him so unable to arrange his own life?

Or was he simply seeing plots where none existed?

That must be it. He was simply being thin-skinned about the matter. He had, after all, never seen the ladies of London run from him, and his brothers must know that. And he was not going to botch this wedding.

Not at all.

He was going to make this day a perfect one for Eleanor. And then tomorrow, he was going to marry her. And she would be happy and that would be that.

With that determined, he started down the steps, heading for his place at the starting line to begin the race. The sound of the front doors opening, and his father's gruff complaints, made him stop and turn.

"Stop swinging the damned chair. Hold it steady. Now, easy down the steps. Take them together, you fools. Do you want to tip me out? Just put me down! Put me down! Bellows can wheel me about from here."

Irritation kindled in an instant in Geoff and he strode to his father's side. "What is this, some miraculous recovery? Or do you wish to be able to lay the blame of your collapse on Eleanor's race?"

The Earl glanced up at his son as the two burly footmen who had carried him out in his Bath-chair hurried to tuck the wool rug around his legs and settle him more comfortably. "You are impertinent, lad. Oh, leave off, you fools." He waved away the footmen, then turned to his son. "And you may have arranged all this for that Glover girl, but, by God, I am still Earl here. And I should be a damn poor one not to make even an appearance for our guests."

Geoff's eyes narrowed and he pressed his mouth into a tight line to keep back further argument. With his father in this mood, he could only succeed in stoking the Earl's stubborn determination to do as he pleased. The Earl's skin was pale, but not overly white, and he looked alert enough. Geoff glanced again at his father's shaking hands and hunched shoulders, and vague, uneasy doubts tickled at the back of his mind, but he had no time to sort through those stray thoughts.

Abruptly, he turned to Bellows. "Fetch Dr. Ibbotson from over there by the pasture gate." He glanced back to his father. "Given Ibbotson's assessment of your condition, I take it that you have no objection to having him close to hand?"

Fire kindled in the Earl's eyes. He opened his mouth as if to say something, but then he seemed to change his mind. He sank deeper into his chair, folding his hands under the rug. "Fetch Ibbotson if you must, and then you may go and start this race of yours. Or do you mean to wait until dark and hold it by candlelight?"

After a nod to Bellows to get the doctor, Geoffrey turned away, striding to the starting line. He had to stop along the way to talk with others, and force smiles that he did not feel.

Finally, he reached the white tape held by two of the grooms. Tully handed him the pistol that he had readied, loaded with powder but no shot.

"On your marks, gentlemen," Geoff called to the riders.

As the grooms stretched out the white tape, Geoff glanced around to find Dr. Ibbottson now beside the Earl, bending down and looking doubtful as the Earl spoke to him. That conversation sparked a fresh wave of uneasiness in Geoff, but he put his attention on the race at hand and his current responsibilities.

He glanced at Squire Boscomb. The man gave him a nod, and his dark horse danced under a tightened rein.

The crowd quieted as the Squire called out the course again to the riders—out through the home woods to the village church, then south across fields to the spire of the old Norman watch tower, and then back again to Westerley.

"The winner shall be the first man back to catch the flag," the Squire said, gesturing to where one of the grooms had just planted a flag that snapped in the wind, showing the Westerley coat of arms, a white castle and a crouching griffin on a blue field. "Now, up to the line, gentlemen."

The riders crowded their horses forwards to the tape. The younger, more daring rode in their shirtsleeves and waistcoats, but two of the older gentlemen had on their scarlet hunting coats. Puffs of steam rose from the horses' nostrils, and from their warm, quivering flanks. Their hooves stamped the cold ground with impatience.

Geoff glanced around once more, wondering where Eleanor was in this crowd. Then he lifted the pistol into the air and pulled the trigger.

The report echoed, a billow of brimstone-smoke rose. The white tape fluttered to the ground and ten horses burst forward.

As the horses galloped away, the crowd surged forward, yelling encouragement to their favorites, crying taunts to Squire Boscomb that he had been left behind, and cheering just for the sake of making noise.

Paying little heed to this, Geoff glanced around once more for Eleanor. Had she a good view of the race? This was her event and she ought to enjoy it. Oh, where the devil was she?

The cheers and noise faded as the horses thundered into the home woods and were lost to view for the moment. Some in the crowd had brought spyglasses with them, and now they trained them for a flash of coat color to see who led the field. Others climbed onto their carriages for a better view.

"Dunleigh's down," someone yelled. "But that red horse of his is still with the leaders."

Geoff ignored the comment. Frustration simmered inside him, along with worry. Had Eleanor's skittishness in crowds frightened her away? Was she somewhere cowering and terrified?

And then he saw her, standing precariously on the back of a wagon whose horses danced in their harness from the excitement around them. Andrew stood on the ground next to her, and as Geoff watched, his brother put a steadying hand up to Eleanor's waist.

The leash he had held over his temper through all else that day snapped. Jaw set, he strode to where his brother was so casually endangering and fondling his bride.

Fourteen

Eleanor clapped her hands and bounced a little on the wagon, hardly aware of how it shifted below her, or of the hand at her waist that steadied her. She had not realized the race would be so thrilling. She could just make out the dark, tall shape of Squire Boscomb's horse, somewhere towards the front. And she could see the flash of bright red of the riderless red horse—poor Mr. Dunleigh would have a long walk back. The small gray, as Andrew had predicted, fought for the lead along with a tall bay, who seemed to almost disappear as the sky darkened and the horses reached the spire of the village church and vanished for the moment.

"I cannot see them now," Eleanor said, straining, standing on tiptoe.

And then a sharp voice cut into her enjoyment. "Of all the idiot notions. Get her down from there before she breaks her neck. That team could bolt at any moment."

Startled, Eleanor glanced down into Lord Staines's scowling face, a little irritated that now he should choose to give her some of his attention and resenting that his only words for her were harsh condemnation. Cynthia Cheeverly had at least gotten smiles.

Turning from him, she stretched on tiptoe again for a

better view and waved away his concern. "Don't be silly. I could always jump clear if they did shy."

In the next instant, strong arms swept her off the wagon and she found herself set firmly back on the ground.

Her temper fired and she jerked away from his touch. "Is that the only way you can handle a woman—by mauling her?"

Putting a gloved hand over her mouth, she stepped back. Oh, why had she said that to him? She not meant to. It had simply come out.

For an instant, his eyes clouded. Then he turned to his brother, his face setting into austere lines that made him look as if carved from marble. "I shall have a word with you later about this. Eleanor, come along. You can see the end of the race from the finish line, and then you have a duty to hand out the silver tray to the winner. You can do that, can you not?"

He stretched out his hand to her.

Anger at the unfairness of it all fired in her, sudden and hot, mixing uncomfortably with her stinging shame for the ill-mannered words she had thrown at him. But those few words had not even touched him. Nothing hurt him. Nothing reached him. He had walled himself off from everyone, except from his precious Cynthia, who did not want him. It was all so very unfair.

"I'll escort her," Andrew said, stepping forward. "No need for you to worry."

Staines shot his brother a warning glance. "I think you have done enough today. Eleanor?"

He stood there, his hand out to her.

Lifting her chin, she turned to Andrew. "Thank you for your company. You made the day such a pleasure for me." She glanced at Staines's hand, and then looked up to meet his cold stare. "You need not feel obliged to offer me your company. I know what is expected of me—and we have made our agreement, have we not? So you do not have to spend any time with me more than is utterly necessary."

She turned and strode away before she could lose her courage. Her heart pounded in sick, fast thuds in her throat and her skin burned. But she did not care if he thought her a shrew. She was unhappy with him and she wanted him to know it. And if this made him want to cry off marrying her at this late date, well, so much the better, she thought, her eyes stinging and her throat tight.

Blindly, she found her way to the flag at the finish.

Cheering began to build around them—the horses had rounded the Norman watch tower on the hill south of Westerley and the deep thud of iron-shod hoofs on the turf grew louder, like approaching thunder in the ground, as the riders galloped for the finish. She cheered and clapped without knowing who had won the race as the horses thundered past in a close grouping.

It was Bellows who handed her the silver tray to bestow upon the winner, and she did so, realizing then that Mr. Josiah's gray gelding had won the race, and that his rider seemed delighted with his victory.

Two things struck her at once as she glanced around herself, forgetting her misery. It occurred to her that, despite the cold, everyone seemed to have enjoyed the day. Money changed hands as winners collected on their bets. Tankards were lifted to drink to the riders' health. And she could hear talk starting of who might enter the next race. The day had been a success. And with a small shock she realized she had not thought once of her fear of crowds.

Then the misery returned full force for she knew why she did not mind the press of people about her. Scan the crowd as she did now, she could not catch even a glimpse of him. And the crowded lawn seemed desperately empty without him there.

She had indeed learned how not to care what others

thought of her. But now she cared too much for one cold-hearted man.

Stopping before the mirror in the hall, Geoff frowned at his image. His black evening clothes made him look a more likely parson than Andrew, but he could not help that. Tonight, he needed to play his role as the Earl of Herndon's son and heir for the tenants' and servants' ball. And he needed to play it better than he had done so this afternoon.

His cheeks warmed with the memory of how badly he had acted toward Eleanor. After she had stormed off, Andrew had wasted no time in telling him that he had never before been ashamed of his own brother. When Geoff had fired back that he simply had a concern for his bride, Andrew had glared at him and said, "Well, you have a damn strange way of showing it. And it would serve you right if that display of such concern decides her not to marry you!" And then he turned and strode away, leaving Geoff too sullen to go after either of them.

His anger had long since faded, leaving behind only the uncomfortable guilt that Andrew had been right. He had acted badly, and could find no reason for it other than to think it had to be the strain of his approaching wedding. Yes, that had to be it. Coupled with having to deal with his father and too many house guests, and Cynthia, and everything else. Devil take it, what man wouldn't have his temper shortened?

He glowered at his own image, thinking of the easy smiles that Eleanor had given to his brother. Devil take her, perhaps she ought to marry Andrew if she had more care for him than for anyone else.

Turning from the mirror, he started down the stairs again.

The hall's feudal glory shone best at Christmas, decked

as it was in seasonal splendor. Green pine garlands draped the walls. Clumps of holly—red berries glistening in the dark, spiky leaves—hung over the mantel and the lintels. The spices of wassail—of mulled wine and hot cider— laced the air, mixing with the smoke from the yew logs laid on the fire in the great hall. A cold supper of ham, goose, beef, mutton, jellies, puddings, cakes, pastries, and fruit from the greenhouse would be laid out in the billiard room and in the drawing room as well.

He would hand out pennies to the children, and braces of pheasant or woodcock to his tenants. The dancing— lively jigs and rowdy reels—would go on until four or five in the morning. And the guests would all wish him happy Christmas and blessings for his wedding day, and he would have to look as if he had known what the devil he had been doing when he had asked Eleanor Glover to marry him.

The kissing bough he had plucked for her hung above the double-doors, between the hall and the drawing room, that had been thrown open to allow guests to pass easily between the hall and its dancing and the other rooms. He gave the doors, and the mistletoe a wide berth, and headed to the library to pour himself a fortifying brandy.

Lord, had there ever been a more miserable bride-groom?

He had acted a dolt today, spoiling her steeplechase instead of making it a pleasure as he had promised himself. So how could he make it up to her? Apologize? Explain himself? How did he do either of those things without telling her the truth and driving her away?

I am sorry, Eleanor, but you are about to marry a fellow who is a heartless bastard.

No, for better or worse, he had made a bargain with Eleanor, and he might be a devil of a fellow, but he had never broken his word to anyone. Their agreement had been sealed by this race of hers—a token given and pledged.

He stopped suddenly with the brandy glass to his lips.

Devil take it, the damn ring. Another token to exchange tomorrow. Where was Patrick with the ring?

He started out of the library, determined to find his brother. Had Patrick been unable to come up with a replacement, and so made himself scarce? Would he have to fetch another ill-fitting ring from the family jewels? Eleanor deserved better than that. But she deserved better than him, as well. However, she was going to get him on the morrow. And whatever ring he could produce.

Geoff found his brother still in his rooms, struggling to tie a decent cravat.

"If you did not come back with a ring, you may slip a strangling knot into it and save us both some time," Geoff said, shutting the door behind him.

Patrick let out a muffled curse, then threw up his hands. With another oath he began to rip the white linen from around his neck. "That's the third I've ruined. And there's your dashed ring for you. Two, in fact. On the dresser next to my brushes. Patterson, bring me another neck-cloth."

Geoff moved at once to the dresser, as Patrick's valet brought out another strip of starched white linen.

"Which box?" Geoff asked, eyeing the three black boxes that bore the mark of Findlay and Finch, each tied with a gold satin ribbon.

Patrick lifted his chin and began the process of wrapping the starched linen around his neck collar again. "The square ones are yours. Findlay seemed to think one of them just the thing, but he could not agree with Finch's choice, so I carted both their rings home."

He paused to tie the ends of his cravat and then lowered his chin, creasing folds into place.

After a critical glance at his reflection and a frustrated

sigh, he turned to his brother. "Besides, I felt a good deal more comfortable having a second string to my bow this time, I can tell you."

Pulling the ribbon off one box, Geoff opened it and studied the ring nestled in velvet inside. It was a square-cut diamond. Simple. Elegant. More square diamonds fit around the band. It was something he might have chosen for Cynthia, Geoff thought, a touch uncomfortable with it. It looked too large for Eleanor's slender hands. Closing the box, he set it aside and opened the second box, and then frowned even more.

Light glittered off a deep yellow, pear-cut stone. A topaz, he thought, ready to close the box and tell Patrick this trinket would never do. But then brilliant blues flashed in the stone. He twisted it in the light, watching the depth of colors dazzle in the candlelight.

Shrugging into his coat, Patrick came over to his side. "Pretty ain't it? Yellow diamond, Findlay said. Fellow went on about how Miss Glover's a rare lady herself. Thought it looked a bit like a rather good sherry, myself."

Geoff pulled his attention away from the glittering stone. He fit the lid back on the box and then glanced at the third, small oblong black box on Patrick's mahogany dresser. "And what is that?"

"That? Something Eleanor ordered. I promised Findlay to give it her. Probably a present for the wedding or Christmas, and no doubt meant for you, so don't you go prying."

Geoff's fingers itched to do just that, but he gave his brother a disdainful glance. "I am a little above the age of uncontrollable curiosity. Now you may take your coat off again. You look as if you have slept-upon-sheets wrapped around your neck. Patterson, another neckcloth please."

Putting down his boxes, Geoff went to his brother and undid the cravat that Patrick had tied. Patrick grumbled, but submitted. When he finished, Geoff surveyed his handiwork with a good deal more satisfaction than he would have expected. It felt good to do something for someone else, and to stop worrying his own problems for a bit.

"I say, Geoff, awfully decent of you to do this," Patrick said, eyeing the intricate tying of his cravat.

Geoff lifted the corner of his mouth in a smile. "Your reward for not losing a second ring—or a third. I'll take them both, and this down to Eleanor as well," he said, gathering up the boxes from Findlay and Finch.

"Mind you, no sneaking a glimpse," Patrick called out.

Shooting him a scornful glance, Geoff left the room. He took the rings to his own room, and then tucked the other slim box into his waistcoat pocket and went in search of Eleanor.

Guests had begun to arrive. The hum of voices, spiked by laughter, echoed up from the hall. He hoped that Andrew had been on hand to greet everyone, for the Earl would not be downstairs tonight. Geoff had seen to that himself, arranging with Bellows to slip a few drops of laudanum into the glass of wine that the Earl took with his dinner.

The Earl had, of course, insisted that he would attend the wedding on the next day. But Geoff intended that his father would at least rest himself tonight. Even Ibbottson had frowned at how the Earl had spent most of the day overextending himself.

In fact, Geoff had seen Ibbottson and the Earl together that afternoon, Ibbottson's portly figure hunched and bent as he seemed to be giving the Earl a right proper lecture about something. Surprisingly, the Earl had even looked a touch guilty, and for an instant that afternoon Geoff's neck had tingled with the suspicion that those two had been plotting something. Those misgivings haunted him as he descended the stairs.

Then he saw her and he forgot all else.

He had never thought Eleanor particularly pretty. He had been right—tonight she was beautiful. An inner glow lit her face. It charged her brown eyes with golden sparks. It animated her features, making it impossible for him to drag his stare from her face. The stray wisps of sable brown hair made a halo around her face.

She stood in the center of a half-circle of children, a mixed lot of gentry and yeoman, but all of them made quiet by some magic of her own. Their parents—neighbors and farmers, relatives and friends—he noted only as voices in the background, an interference that left him unable to hear her story. From her intent expression and gestures, he gathered that she was weaving some sort of tale.

She acted out the parts, frowning and smiling and making outrageous faces that had the children giggling and then going still with suspense, their mouths agape and their eyes huge.

Like a Christmas fool himself, he realized he was still standing on the stairs, an odd ache in his chest. For a moment he could not place the emotion—and then it struck him. He was jealous. But that was utterly absurd. Jealous of some half-dozen farmers' brats, and a few neighbors' children? It was just more nerves about this wedding, that was all.

She is just a girl. A sensible girl who will make a sensible wife, and who does not mind if I cannot love her.

But inside his chest, a burning, twisting ache wrapped around his heart that she would never look at him with such warmth glowing in her eyes.

He stepped down the few remaining stairs and moved at once to greet his guests, looking anywhere but at Eleanor—at the woman who would become his wife on the morrow. The woman who would share his life, and nothing else with him. That was their bargain, after all, was it not? Oh, what the devil had he gotten himself into with all these promises to her and his father and everyone else?

As Geoffrey moved to greet his neighbors, Eleanor stumbled in her tale. The children did not seem to mind. She was telling them a Christmas story, about Mary and Joseph's flight into Egypt to escape King Herod. Now, she looked up at Geoffrey . . . at Lord Staines—so calm, so distant—and her glance snagged on his and tripped her thought into chaos.

She had known the instant he had appeared. Not from the reaction of those around her, for the children and the guests seemed to pay no heed to his arrival. No, she knew by the fiery awareness that swept over her skin.

How terribly unfair love was that it should leave her so aware of him. So vulnerable. She needed armor, but instead she seemed only to become ever more sensitive to his presence, to his moods, to his very being.

Her story ended and the children crowded around her and begged for another, but their elders came to remind them of duties to sing carols for the house. They did so, lining up before the ancient fireplace, with its crackling Yule log. Their voices rambled over the notes rather like wild sheep over an open meadow.

Eleanor listened, entranced and charmed.

"They make up for quality with volume," Lord Staines said, leaning close to whisper in her ear.

She had felt the warmth of him close upon her as he stepped near, so she had not been startled by his words. But a fierce need to defend these innocents against his cynical scorn rose in her.

"Their enthusiasm is treat enough, is it not?" she said.

"Ah, but that never endures. Now does it?"

His curt tone surprised her, and she rounded on him, ready to take him to task for such cynicism, and for so rudely pushing away this gift of song from children's voices. But the singing ended, and the warm applause that rewarded their efforts left Eleanor with no need to champion their efforts. She stared at Lord Staines instead, and found him holding out his hand to her, his gaze stern.

"Come. We must open the dancing. I promise I shall not burden you with more than this one dance. Patrick is by far the most light-footed one in the family."

She said nothing in answer, but laid her hand on the back of his, her fingers chilled, and allowed him to lead her to the center of the hall, all too aware that everyone watched them. She wet her lips and tried not to be nervous.

The furnishings had been cleared, leaving the hall vast and long. At the far end, near the front door, the farmers with musical inclination had assembled on the entrance steps to make up a small orchestra. She noted two violins, a guitar, and a penny whistle player in the group. They struck up a lively jig.

Despite his words, she knew him as a good dancer, and the dance was one that anyone could manage. They danced long-wise in a country set, the tune brisk. Lord Staines led her to the top of the set, then his brother, Andrew, led Elizabeth out, and Patrick took up the dance with Emma, and others joined in.

Arm turns, and then a "hay," with women and men weaving in and out of the pattern like a weaver's shuttle. Bows and curtseys, good-natured grins. His hand always seemed to be there for her to grasp, his touch leading her through the movements, his face before her, so devastatingly handsome.

When the music ended, Eleanor could not stop from smiling up at him, for he made it so easy to dance. So wonderful. For a long moment, he looked back down at her, his face relaxed and nearly smiling, and her heart did a small turn.

No, don't do that. He does not want love from you, she thought, panic wrapping around her chest and squeezing out all the pleasure of a moment ago. She stiffened and his smile faded as he looked away and tugged down his waistcoat even though it had not a wrinkle in it to smooth.

The musicians struck up another tune, but Lord Staines led her away from the center of the hall. She cast a longing glance back, and then looked down at the bare, stone floor as he led her toward the drawing room's wide, double-doorway.

He paused with her there. "I'm sorry to take you from the festivities, but . . . well, here. Patrick brought this for you from Guildford." He pulled a small, narrow box from his waistcoat pocket and thrust it into her hands.

She glanced at it, delight catching her by surprise. "For me? What is it?"

"Don't you know? Patrick said you had ordered it from Findlay and Firth."

Her delight collapsed as she realized it was not a gift from him, but the watch chain and the locket she had ordered. She tried to prop her smile back into place. "Oh, yes. Of course. They did promise me a . . . well, a locket I asked them to make."

The shaft of disappointment startled him. So it was not a Christmas gift for him, nor even a wedding gift. Well, why should she buy anything for him? He had nothing to give her, other than a wedding ring.

Feeling childishly slighted—and hating himself for it— he sought for something pleasant to say to her to make up for how badly he seemed to keep acting with her. Devil take it, but where was his much vaulted charm with women now?

"Thank you," she said, looking up at him, her skin still rosy from the dance. Candlelight drew warm lights from her soft brown hair.

For a moment, temptation rose in him to lean down and brush his lips across hers. Such a simple gesture. But would she take it, meant as it was, as a gesture of friendship and naught else?

He frowned at her. "You ought to thank Patrick. I have done nothing—not one thing—for you, other than to be a perfect oaf."

"That's not true. You . . . you gave me what I asked for."

His mouth twisted. "A steeplechase. A fine thing for a gentleman to give his bride."

Cheeks burning, she stared down at the box in her hands. "I thought . . . well, it was what I asked for."

He put a finger under her chin and lifted her face. "Yes. What you asked for. But I wonder at times, Eleanor, what you first wrote on that card that you then crossed out? What else do you want from life, Eleanor?"

Entranced by his gaze, by the velvet in his voice, by the touch of his hand on her chin, she could not move. Heart pounding, she parted her lips, the truth trembling inside her.

"I . . . I want. . . ."

She hesitated as the music dropped away, and then a voice raised above hers and the others around them, "Look, my Lord Staines has caught his bride under the mistletoe!"

Fifteen

Eleanor glanced up, her head suddenly light. There, over the doorway, dangled the pale, round green leaves with the waxy white berries. They indeed stood under the kissing bough.

Someone whistled. Someone else called for Lord Staines to kiss his bride proper. Eleanor could only stand there, frozen, her heart pounding and her breath quickening, wishing that she could melt into nothing.

Please, no, she thought with desperation.

Staines kept her chin caught between his thumb and forefinger so that her face remained turned up to his. Trembling now, she stared up at him, silent pleading in her eyes for him to let her go. She still could walk slowly away, but if she had to stand there much longer with everyone looking at her, she would bolt and run and disgrace herself, him, and her family by acting like a frightened child.

His eyes clouded, and then his thumb caressed her chin. She shuddered and closed her eyes.

He only said her name. Once. Soft as the memory of a breeze. "Eleanor."

She let out a sigh at the sound of her name on his lips. *I will pretend he loves me. That he cares. For it is the only way I can get through this.*

And then his breath warmed her cheek. His lips touched hers. A light whisper. She wanted to cling to that warmth, that promise, that hint of something more. She still trembled, but no longer from fear. Her own breath came out in a soft sigh, and her eyes fluttered open.

For an instant, she thought she saw a softening in his eyes. A momentary flicker of some feeling. His pupils widened, darkening his eyes into endless depths. But then that cold reserve slipped back, and she became aware of the clapping hands, the smiles, the crowd thickening around them.

"Excuse me," she muttered, unable to control herself an instant longer. She turned away and pushed through the crowd towards the stairs. Elizabeth called after her, but she could not stop. Running now, she fled up the stairs and into her own room where she could shut the door on the people and the stares and the panic.

A moment later, when her heart had almost slowed to a normal pace, someone rapped on the door. "Ellie? It's me, Elizabeth."

Eleanor turned and leaned her cheek on the cool, hard wood. She forced a bright tone. "I'm fine. Really. It was just . . . you know how I am with crowds. Will you make my regrets? Tell them . . . tell them I have the migraine."

"Do you want me to sit with you for a bit?"

"No," Eleanor said, too quickly. "No, please. I just wish to be alone for awhile. I shall be fine."

"Very well. But Emma and I shall come see you in the morning to help you dress. Sleep well, Ellie."

Eleanor waited until she had heard Elizabeth's light steps fade. Then she went to her bed and sank onto it. Dear Lord, could this evening get any worse? She glanced down at the box in her hands, only now remembering it, and then she dragged the ribbon off it and opened it.

She almost laughed. Of course. That had to go wrong as well.

Instead of making a watch chain and a glass locket with her mistletoe, the jeweler had made the two items into one. Eleanor stared in dismay at the watch chain with the sphere on the end that forever trapped the mistletoe berry in glass. Almost, she wanted to throw it against the marble fireplace and see it shatter.

And when the berry is gone, there should be no more kissing.

The superstition Geoffrey had told her echoed in her mind. Lifting the box, she clutched it tight to her chest. If she had any sense, she would not believe such nonsense. But love, it seemed, had little to do with sense. And so she tucked the box under her pillow to keep it safe, knowing full well that it was a gift she could never give for it would reveal too much of her hope . . . and her love for him.

Eleanor dreamed of kisses under the mistletoe. Soft, sighing kisses. Deeper kisses that set her pulse fluttering. Teasing kisses that had her body aching with nameless longing.

Half-waking, a smile curved her lips and she stretched. Her feather bed wove a cocoon of warmth that made her want to stay there, drifting in dreams. Church bells tumbled a distant, echoing ringing. *It's Sunday, and Christmas Eve,* she thought, her mind still half-drifting in sleep.

Then she sat bolt upright.

It was her wedding day, and those bells rang for her and Lord Staines.

Her stomach knotted even though she had nothing to worry over. If everything went wrong, she would not marry and perhaps that might be the best for all. So it should not matter to her what happened. Still, she found her hands shaking as she struggled out of bed.

A rumbling rattled her windows, and she glanced towards the dark glass.

Thunder.

Shivering, she ran barefoot to the window and pulled back the velvet drapery. The clouds lay so thick that not even a sliver of dawn streaked the eastern sky. Fat rain drops spattered against the glass. A stormy day for a stormy wedding, she thought, frowning at the darkness.

A soft knock on the door made her turn, and then her maid bustled in, balancing a tray with a rack of toast, a pot of tea, and a bright candle. Elizabeth and Emma came in just after her, already dressed, glowing with excitement, and chattering about the wedding.

Her sisters came to hug her as the maid settled the tray on the bed and then went to light the fire. And then Elizabeth and Emma pulled open the wardrobe and began the job of dressing her.

With no appetite, and little to do, Eleanor sat down beside her bed, next to her rabbit, Bother, who huddled in his crate, and she wished she could copy his actions. But she sipped her tea and watched her sisters shake out her wedding gown—a pale, ice-blue satin. They set out her white shoes and the pale-blue bonnet with its Brussels lace veil that she was to wear. Thunder rumbled again and Eleanor decided she would probably look like a dripping icicle by the time she had walked to the Westerley chapel.

Yawning, still in her night clothes, Evelyn stumbled into the room and curled up on the rug next to Eleanor's chair, close enough to pet Bother. "Are you excited?" she asked.

Eleanor nodded. "And nervous."

"And happy?" Elizabeth asked, smoothing a pair of elbow length white kid gloves.

"I shall be happy when this is all over," Eleanor said, getting to her feet. Evelyn stole into Eleanor's vacated chair, picking up the cowering Bother to hold and stroke.

Elizabeth frowned at Eleanor's comment, but Emma came forward and gave her sister another hug. "Of course you will, because then you shall have a wonderful wedding breakfast, and a splendid day. I must say, your steeplechase was not as bad as I thought it would be, although I still think it a pitiful waste of your card. Now, do you wear the stockings shot with gold, or do you wish to borrow mine with the silver leaves on them?"

Eleanor suggested the gold, but Elizabeth and Emma both overruled her and said the silver would look better. Not that anyone will see them, Eleanor thought. But she soon found herself being dressed as if she were a doll.

Her gown—made in London for far too much money, Eleanor thought—could not be changed, but Emma and Elizabeth found plenty to argue over in the choice of jewelry, what flowers to carry, and how to dress Eleanor's hair. With Bother on her lap, Evelyn simply sat in her nightclothes and rolled her eyes at such fuss, and vowed to elope when it came her turn to wed.

"As if anyone would have you, imp," Emma said.

Evelyn stuck her tongue out at her sister.

"Really, Evelyn," Lady Rushton said, arriving just in time to see this unladylike display. She handed Eleanor a bouquet of forced narcissi, hyacinth, and hothouse camellias, which settled the issue of what flowers Eleanor would carry. Then she shooed Evelyn out to go and dress herself, and took command.

"No, Eleanor will not wear diamonds, Emma. She is going to chapel to marry, not to a ball. You shall wear the pearls I wore when I married your father, dear. And Elizabeth, what have you done, putting her hair in all those braids? We must do something simple that will not spring out into its own life in this damp."

In less than half an hour, Lady Rushton had Eleanor organized, dressed, and downstairs. She had arranged for footmen with umbrellas to walk with them to the chapel, an ancient structure that stood separate at the north end of the main house.

Eleanor glanced around, then asked, "Where is Lord Staines?"

"It is bad luck for him to see you before the ceremony," Emma scolded. Then she took Eleanor's shoulders and faced her toward the hall mirror. "Now, look once for good luck. But only once. Twice is both vain and a bad omen."

Lady Rushton glanced at the watch pinned to her deep blue velvet gown. "Oh, where is Evelyn? And your father? He went upstairs to assist Lord Herndon, and I have not seen anything of him since. I am certain Lord Staines will be on time, but I vow that your father will be late to his own funeral!"

Just as she spoke, Evelyn came running down the stairs, her bonnet untied and clutched to her head, her white gown rumpled and its ribbons streaming. "Father says to go on ahead, and he shall come over with Lord Staines and his brothers."

"Oh, very well. Now, mind you, Ellie, put on your pattens to keep your slippers out of the wet. Evelyn, dear, hold still while I finish tying your ribbons."

With her feet in the wooden pattens, which fit around her slippers, Eleanor tottered towards the door, feeling more likely to trip on the awkward clogs and go face first into the mud. But her mother was there by her side, an arm around her waist with a reassuring squeeze.

"It will all be wonderful, darling," Lady Rushton said, and then gave Eleanor a kiss on the cheek. "All weddings are."

Then they were hurrying through the rain to the chapel. Not making the dignified parade that they ought to, but rushing across the gravel drive and into the ancient stone building.

From a window on the second storey of the house, the

Earl watched the parade of umbrellas chase across the lawn. The rain blurred his view, but he caught a glimpse of pale gowns and assumed the bride had taken her place. He gave a snort of disgust. In his day, he wed his bride after a proper walk through the village to the church. And it had been a fine, blustery spring day for that proper procession.

However, the choice of weather was as much his fault as anyone's, for he had pushed for this Christmas wedding date.

Twisting around in his wheeled chair, he glared at Lord Rushton. "Well, they have gone to the chapel, so it must be time for the deed to be done."

Rushton pulled the watch from his waistcoat pocket, glanced at it and then put it away again. "You sound as glum as the sky looks. Is this not what you wanted? What we all want, in fact? Just keep thinking of the grandchildren we shall both soon have."

The Earl's lined face lightened with a momentary smile, but then he fell back to brooding. "That assumes your daughter won't turn missish about the getting of them."

"If you think that, you have not seen enough of how my Ellie looks at your son. And I don't see a man with your son's reputation having any trouble courting his wife. But none of this can happen if we don't get them properly tied, so come along, old friend, and let us give the women a reason to have a good sentimental cry."

Rushton moved behind the Earl's chair and began to wheel it forward, but as they reached the door, a knock sounded and then Bellows ushered in Dr. Ibbottson.

"Ah, Dr. Ibbottson. Come for the wedding, or to see your impatient patient here?" Rushton said, moving around the chair to shake Ibbottson's hand.

The doctor's fleshy jowls lifted in a brief smile. He wished the gentlemen a good day, but then he turned to the Earl. "If I might just have a moment of your time, my lord."

The Earl waved Rushton away, telling him, "Go on, Edward. Don't want your gel fretting. I shall be there in a moment. Go and make certain they do not start without me."

"As if they could," Rushton said, and then left with the butler.

The Earl turned to his doctor. "Well, what word do you want? Another caution for me not to be too active today? Or more of the same prattle as you gave me yesterday?"

Ibbottson frowned and rubbed at the gray stubble on his cheek. "I did nothing last night but think about this day, and our conversation yesterday."

"Not another attack of conscience, man. I thought we sorted that out already."

"No, my lord. You sorted, and I—to my shame—allowed you. But I cannot continue in this. Not after seeing Lord Staines with that poor girl yesterday. And not after seeing that he is not yet over his other attachment. I do agree with you that that infatuation could not have prospered, but still it is a bar between him and beginning anything else."

"Bah. She is married, and he will soon be and that is enough."

Ibbottson straightened his bulky form. "No, my lord. It is not. I allowed you yesterday—and once before that—to convince me that this arrangement could work. But you argue logic when what I have seen are two people who do not have the temperament to conduct this marriage as the business affair you wish it to be. You are playing with the human heart, my lord. And it is to my shame that I let you persuade me that no one's feelings would be bruised."

Glaring at the man, the Earl leaned forward in his chair. "What is this? You want more from me? Is that it?"

"What I want more is for the truth to be told, my lord. But I am still bound by my word to you not to speak of this, and so I ask you again that you release me from that pledge of silence. Or tell Lord Staines yourself the whole of it. Then if he marries, this ceremony can take place without that cloud of deception over it."

"Deception! I tell you, sir, the only deceiving going on is your own in thinking that any good will come of telling all at this stage of the game. She is not all I would have wanted in a daughter, but I'll make do with her."

"You will? And what will your son do when he learns that he has been manipulated? Will he be a happy husband who seeks his wife's bed?"

The Earl hunched down in his chair and glared at Ibbottson. "He'll do as he's bid and get me grandsons!"

Ibbottson's watery eyes narrowed. "Your son, my lord, is as stubborn as yourself. You ought to think a moment and consider what you would do if the tables were turned?"

For a moment, the Earl's eyes blazed. His mouth worked as if chewing on the next words he would spit out. He glared at Ibbottson, but the doctor stared back, his gaze hard and certain.

The Earl's stare was the first to waver. He glanced away and fussed with the rug that lay on his lap. "I cannot tell him. It will do no good now."

"And is that how you keep your promise to the late Countess to ensure your sons' happiness?"

The Earl's eyes glittered as he glared at Ibbottson again. "You dare bring Amanda into this again, and I'll horsewhip you through the village. Oh, devil take you! If this does not go well, I shall ruin you! Now ring for Bellows. Tell him to bring my son up . . . no, better still, tell him to have Staines wait upon me in the drawing room. And God help us all if this goes wrong!"

* * *

"You look as if you could use this," Andrew said, coming up with two glasses in his hand.

Geoff took one of the glasses of amber liquid. Brandy fumes, strong and potent, wove around him. His empty stomach gave a lurch, but he tossed back the brandy and let it burn a path down his throat and into his stomach.

"Afraid I shall not be steady enough?" he asked.

Andrew gave him a smile. "More like that you'll be as stiff as one of those carved effigies in the chapel. Will you stop fretting over what Father wants with you. He no doubt intends to offer some paternal advice, and then to demand a schedule for how soon you will produce some offspring."

"Thank you. It soothes me no end to start thinking of having to set up my nursery," Geoff said, glaring at his brother.

Andrew offered back a grin as Patrick strode into the drawing room.

Glancing at his brothers and the glasses of brandy in their hands, he lifted an eyebrow. "A little early to celebrate, is it not?"

Setting his glass down, Geoff straightened the already straight coat cuffs of his buff-velvet jacket, and then he smoothed his heavy brocade waistcoat. He wished he could sit down, but his gold satin knee breeches had been cut to show off his figure, not for comfort.

"Devil take it, but is Father going to keep us waiting all day?" he muttered.

Andrew shrugged. "Do you think he found out about what you put in his wine last night?"

A querulous voice answered from the doorway. "What do you mean what he put in my wine?"

The brothers turned towards the entrance. Patrick's jaw dropped. Andrew spilt his brandy, staining the leg of his white satin knee breeches. Geoff stood still, his eyes narrowed and the pulse pounding in his clenched jaw.

In the doorway, stood the Earl. He leaned only slightly on an ivory-headed cane, but there was not a sign of any wheeled chair. And while Dr. Ibbottson stood next to him, the Earl seemed quite steady on his own feet. Age had bent his figure, and his right hand shook so that he held the cane with his left. His lined face seemed pale, but no more so than usual, and he glared at his sons, his eyes alert and bright.

"Well, say something," the Earl snapped. "You look like a trio of landed trout. What about that wine?"

Geoff forced his jaw to relax. Then he folded his arms. The back seam of his perfectly cut coat strained across his shoulders, reminding him to try to contain his simmering temper.

Devil take it, but he ought to have known it from the start. His instincts had warned him, but he had put too great a trust in Ibbottson's integrity. He ought to have realized that his father would find a way to bend Ibbottson—and he realized now that that careful letter from the doctor, all the man's words, had said nothing directly about the Earl dying. No, he had offered inferences of limited time, of inevitable consequences to the Earl's past abuse of his health, and warnings that the Earl's shaking palsy was progressing. And he had let Geoff leap to the conclusions that the Earl had wanted.

The only question was how had the Earl finally gotten his way with Ibbottson?

"It seems as if explanations are owed all around," Geoff said, and then shifted his glance to the doctor. "How did he induce you to write that so carefully phrased letter to me? That was a masterpiece, Ibbottson. Not a lie in it. But enough suggestion to have me jumping through the hoops as well."

"What hoops?" Patrick muttered to Andrew, who shushed him.

Eyes narrowing, the Earl came into the room and faced

his eldest son. "Don't blame him. I promised him a hospital in Guildford, endowed with a trust to keep it."

"Ah, I see. Lured him by his own noble intentions. I shall have to remember that trick of using a man's strengths against him."

The Earl glared at him. "If you want to blame him for something, do so for my coming to you now to tell you that I am not dying."

A silence settled into the room.

Geoff stood very still. If he moved, he feared that he would do something violent. Something stupid. So he kept himself utterly still.

Finally, he had control enough of himself to ask, "Why tell me that now? Is it so that there is no need for me to marry that Glover girl if you do not wish it?"

Before the Earl could answer, a movement from the doorway and behind the Earl caught Geoff's attention. He froze, and then the Earl and Ibbottson both turned as well.

Eleanor stood in the doorway, her face as pale as her gown.

Sixteen

Eleanor could only think that Emma had been right—she should not have looked into the mirror a second time.

She had come back to the house, a cloak thrown over her, her pattens crunching on the gravel and a footman hurrying beside her with an umbrella, for something as prosaic as the call of nature. Standing in the cold chapel, she had felt the pressure build in her body, and the fear that she would embarrass herself drove her to whisper to her mother, and then hurry back to the house to find the nearest convenience. Afterwards, she had paused in the hall before donning her pattens and cloak to smooth her hair and her dress, and she had heard the voices from the drawing room.

She had not meant to listen, but the harsh tones had woken a dreadful curiosity in her, drawing her toward the half-open door. And as she stood in the entrance, staring at the Earl and listening to Lord Staines, she thought only what very bad luck she had.

He would have married me, for we had an agreement. She knew that with utter certainty. But now he would not need to, for she could not hold him to something he had been manipulated into doing. He had seen her, so she could not even slip away and pretend that she had not

heard. She could not take the coward's way out, which so
beckoned her.

For a moment, Lord Staines's face darkened, and she
shrank back. But then he forced a smile and held out his
hand to her. "Eleanor, come in. This involves you, so you
might as well hear it."

The Earl glared at his son. "This is not woman's business."

"Until marriage vows do not involve a woman, it certainly is. Eleanor?"

Her steps slow, she came to his side. "I . . . you do not
have to explain. I had not meant to overhear, but . . . well,
perhaps this is how it is meant to end." Looking up into
his face, she tried to memorize the high arch of his cheek-
bone, the curve of his eyebrows, the color of his eyes.
She wanted always to remember how he looked. It would
be all she had.

Then she said, her voice amazingly steady, "I release
you from your promise to marry me, my lord."

The Earl let out a muffled curse. Andrew started to
shake his head, and Patrick let out a low, pained groan.
Lord Staines ignored them. Instead, he stared down at her
with such an intent expression on his face that she could
no longer meet it. Glancing down, she began to fidget
with her gloves, which she had pulled off and not yet put
back on.

He covered her hands with one of his, making her look
up at him again. "It is not just a matter of a promise made.
We shook on an agreement, you and I. That cannot be set
aside."

"But you—"

He cut off her words by laying a finger across her lips.

"I am—I should hope—a man of honor. And what my
father has spoken of is something for me to sort out with
him, but it has no affect on anything between us."

"Of course it does. If you had had more time, you

would not have chosen me!" She heard the desperation seep into her voice and fought not to show such weakness and need.

His mouth twisted down. "How can I answer that? Might I have done different things in different circumstances? Yes, I might—or I might not. Or is this your way of telling me that you do not wish to marry me now?"

That haunted look had come back into his eyes, and it tore at her heart that he must be thinking that she would reject him as Cynthia had done.

"No, that is not it at all," she said, the words falling out too rapidly. She bit down on her lower lip. Why would he not call off this ill-fated match? And yet the tears stung the back of her eyes, ready to fall if he should do so.

He offered a small, stiff smile. "We shall talk more later. But I think we have kept our guests waiting long enough for a wedding."

She nodded, unable to trust her voice.

The rain had lessened, so that the walk to the chapel actually was a walk, not a mad dash through the wet. Once there, Lord Rushton greeted them easily, but Lady Rushton and her other daughters gasped to see Eleanor with Lord Staines. They whisked her aside, muttering about grooms not seeing their brides before the ceremony.

Geoff took his place with Patrick at the altar, and the only thing that stood out in his mind was the sight of Eleanor's pale face as she walked down the aisle to him. Her voice dropped to near a whisper as she said her vows. He muttered his own responses as he ought. And then the vicar pronounced them man and wife, and it was done.

So why did he not feel relief? Why were his shoulders still knotted and his stomach still tensed? Why did the urge to turn and stride out of the church and keep walking away from this make him unable to stand still?

He led Eleanor to the register to sign her name, he signed his after hers. It all seemed rather unreal, and anticlimactic after his father's earlier disclosure. His anger over that had faded, but a simmering sense of betrayal and resentment lay just under his skin, and he did not trust himself to say anything pleasant to the Earl.

This was nothing like what he had imagined his wedding day to be, he thought, as he led Eleanor back to the house and the wedding breakfast. And to endless good wishes for happiness.

"Where are my things?" Eleanor asked, staring blankly around the room she had thought of as hers at Westerley. Numb cold trickled through her fingers. "Never tell me they were moved into the late Countess' rooms?"

The maid stared at her. "Oh, no, my lady. They were moved to the Green bedroom, next to Lord Staines's rooms."

My lady. It was not the first time that day she had been so addressed, but the oddness of it left her unsettled. *My lady.* She folded a pleat of the white gown that she had changed into for dinner that evening. The day had at last wound down. The breakfast had ended. Most of the wedding guests had departed, but a few members of the Westerley family had stayed on for Christmas Eve dinner, and for games of Hunt the Slipper and Snapdragon, with Evelyn and Patrick being the best at snatching the raisins from the brandy flames. Eleanor had forced a smile and joined in, but there was still tomorrow to face, with church to attend, and Christmas dinner with more relatives and neighbors.

Thankfully, Lord Staines had said they were not to go away on a honeymoon, but would stay at Westerley until Twelfth Night. She would have her family with her until then. And she would rather endure an army of Westerleys than have to face awkward days alone with the one she had married.

"Shall I show you the way, my lady?" the maid asked, looking a little worried.

Eleanor thanked her, but said she could find it. Only once in the room, with its pretty green drapery and flowery wallpaper, she found herself eyeing the connecting door as if a tiger lived behind it. Which, given the circumstances, was not that far from true.

Lord Staines had prowled the house all day with a fixed smile in place and his blue eyes crackling. She had seen him exchange words once with his father, but she knew quite well that Lord Staines had not forgiven his father for his interference. Would that be a shadow over her marriage? Or were there so many already that one more did not matter in such darkness?

"I will try to make him happy," she had told the Earl that afternoon.

He had humphed at her and narrowed his eyes in a gesture so like his son that her heart skittered for an instant, but then he had squeezed her hands before turning away.

Andrew and Patrick Westerley had, at least, been very kind. They had claimed the right as brothers to kiss her cheeks, and had gone out of their way to introduce her to all the Westerley cousins and uncles and aunts. And her sisters and her mother had hovered close to her, keeping her distracted with chatter and their own delight. However, it was Lord Staines who had consumed her thoughts and her worries.

He still did.

She drifted through the room, touching the wedding presents that had been left here by the servants, fingering the ribbons on the boxes, glancing at the cards attached and feeling strangely let down. She was not certain what she had expected, but it was not to feel . . . to feel so displaced.

Her maid came in, and after changing from her dress

into her night clothes and a red velvet dressing gown, Eleanor dismissed the girl and then curled up in a chair near the fire with her rabbit on her lap so that she could smooth his long, soft ears.

When would he come to her? Would he come? She desperately hoped so. She wanted this night to be over. At least she would know then that she could be a wife to him in more than name. But her insides wanted to turn upside down at the thought that he would be disappointed with her.

With a sigh, she got up and followed her mother's advice on dealing with her wedding night. She poured herself a glass of wine from the decanter left with two glasses on a side table.

Three glasses later, two hours had passed and still no sign of her husband. She had opened all the presents and had tried to read a book. Even Bother had given up on the late hour, fidgeting so in her lap that she had had to settle him back in his crate. She had no one for company except her own thoughts which darted about like frightened birds in a cage.

Glowering at the porcelain figurine given them by Mr. and Mrs. Cheeverly, she wondered if Geoff lay in his own room now, thinking of Cynthia?

She had watched him watching Mrs. Cheeverly at the wedding breakfast, and that worm of jealousy had crawled loose inside her. She found herself hoping that perhaps her father knew of a parish living that could be given to Mr. Cheeverly that would take him and his wife to Northumberland. But that would only take Mrs. Cheeverly away from sight, and not out of Lord Staines's heart.

Curling up again in the chair beside the dying fire, Eleanor tucked her robe even tighter about her and glanced up at the clock on the mantel. Nearly midnight. Nearly Christmas. She would never forget this Christmas. And then she heard the door open behind her.

She was on her feet in an instant.

He stood in the doorway, so handsome that her heart clenched and a wave of raw longing swept through her. His white lawn shirt lay open at the neck, his cravat and waistcoat had been stripped away. Buff breeches clung to his muscular legs. He would have seemed too intimidating, except that, like a boy on a night lark, he wore white stockings with no slippers or shoes. He had thrown on a blue, silk brocade dressing gown, and it billowed unbelted as he came into the room.

"I did not think you would come," she said. Then she pressed her lips tight together. She had not meant to say anything. It was his choice, after all, to see her or not. She should not scold him.

He frowned and came into the room, stopping to glance at a jewel encrusted box that someone had given them. "You have been busy, opening all this."

Her face warmed. "I beg your pardon. Should I have waited for you?"

He shrugged. "No. You should please yourself in these matters."

A hard lump formed in her throat. She wished now that she had had a fourth glass of wine. The pleasant distancing that the other three glasses had provided seemed to have vanished when he walked into the room. She wondered if she should offer him a drink, then she glanced up at him from under her lashes. His eyes were very bright. Had he been drinking already? Perhaps trying to find desire for her in a bottle?

"Where have you been?" she asked, and then immediately added, "No, I should not have said that. I beg your pardon. I do not want to be an interfering wife. That was the bargain, was it not?"

He came closer to her. Her pulse raced.

"Do not be nervous, Eleanor. I will not hurt you. I will not do anything you do not like."

But the question was, would she be able to do anything that he liked?

He took her hands between his. "You are cold. Did you catch a chill sitting here, waiting?"

She could only shake her head. She did not trust her voice, not with him rubbing her hands between his. She fixed her stare on his hands. So elegant. So warm. So much larger than her own that they engulfed her.

Gently, Geoff reached out and traced the curve of his wife's lips with one finger. It had taken him far too long to work up the courage to come and face her, and still he did not know quite what to do with her.

His wife.

His mouth dried and it took all his concentration to keep his hands steady as he touched her. He knew how to deal with the women of London, but a wife was a new experience to him. This day had been too full of too many new experiences, too many emotions, and not enough time to sort through them. His father's confession, the wedding, having to see Cynthia and accept her wishes for him to be happy with his bride.

Oddly, Cynthia had been the easiest of all of them to handle, and still he did not understand why that should be. He had watched her at the wedding breakfast—who could not watch such a lovely woman? But something was different about her. Or perhaps about him. It was as if he were seeing her for the first time and noting how she smiled at her husband, but with a distance between them. He had always been intrigued by the serene poise with which Cynthia met the world. He had thought of it as a challenge, that some lucky man would find a way to light the fires underneath that cool exterior.

And then the oddest thought had struck him. What if he had never really seen her as she was? What if there were no fires to light? Or what if she did not want them lit?

He had turned away from those thoughts, uncomfortable with them. No, it had been his fault that he could not stir Cynthia's passion. The fault could not be with her. She was too perfect.

Eleanor's fingers trembled as his hand tightened around hers and that brought him back to the moment. He let go of her. He would give her time. He would act a gentleman with his lady wife. He would not make the same mistakes he had made with Cynthia.

Moving away, he picked up a figurine—a country couple who gazed vapidly at each other over a fence railing. "Who gave us this?" he asked, thinking it a useless knick-knack.

"Mr. and Mrs. Cheeverly," she said, her voice so flat that he had to glance at her.

She was not looking at him, but stared into the fire, her arms wrapped around herself. He glanced at the figures again, startled that Cynthia should have picked out such a gift. She usually had such elegant taste. But then he realized that perhaps the appeal of it for her had lain in the safe sentiment shown. He frowned at that thought.

"The woman here rather looks like Cynthia," he said, mostly to say something. And then he put it down, uninterested in the cold, lifeless porcelain. He came back to Eleanor's side.

Dropping her arms, she moved away. He frowned, and stamped down on the edge of impatience that fired in him. Devil take it, but was she going to keep dancing away from him all night? Should he leave? He glanced at her slender fingers, now tugging at the ties to her dressing gown.

Desire slivered through him. He wanted to be doing that.

Go slow, you idiot. It's not as if she's madly in love with you and burning for your touch.

Forcing a smile, he went over to where her rabbit snuggled in his crate. "How fares your patient? Does he like his new rooms?"

That drew her closer. She came to him, as doe-eyed and wary as a wild creature herself. But she came and leaned over the crate next to him, so close that her perfume teased his senses with the aroma of orange blossoms.

"He is much better, thank you. Tully thinks we might take off the splint in a few more days."

With light hands, he checked the animal's injury. "Days? Less, I'd say. You have a healing way with creatures, my Lady Staines."

"Oh, please do not call me that. It makes me feel . . . well, as if I have stolen something that is not mine."

Straightening, he stood and moved his hands from stroking the rabbit to stroking her hands again. "You are not a thief. You are a magician. You have magic in your touch. I've seen you work it with your animals—and with the village children. You had them quiet as church mice the other evening."

She made a face, then moved away again to stand closer to the fire. "The only magic there was a story."

"Then tell me a story," he said, coming closer, sitting down in the winged chair and stretching out his hand to her.

She shook her head, but after a moment's hesitation she came to him and put her hand in his. He drew her down to his lap.

"I have no stories tonight," she said.

"I think you do," he told her, his voice softening. She looked lovely in firelight, with her sable hair down and the fire finding red from its depths. He smoothed a hand over its wispy softness.

"Your lips could tell me many stories," he whispered, and then he tightened his arms around her, feeling her soft curves melt into his demand, determined she would not slip away from him again.

His mistletoe berry was long gone, but that was one superstition he could prove wrong. His kisses would not vanish along with the berry.

Gently, he fit his lips to hers. She sat passive and still in his lap, like a trapped rabbit herself. He let his tongue glide over her lips, and the taste of her sent a jolt through him. He craved more. Tightening his arms around her, he deepened the kiss.

And then he felt her tremble.

He drew back at once, shocked by the heat burning under his skin, aware that she stirred feelings in him that he had never known. He wanted her desperately, he realized.

The pulse beat fast in her throat and her eyes had grown even larger.

I've frightened her, he thought. And suddenly he knew that he would do anything to protect her—even from himself.

With a smile, he forced himself to put her on her feet. Then he stood. The ache for her went straight to his core, but better to be cautious than risk their future together. He could be patient, he told himself, even as his body rebelled against the cold lack of no longer having her in his arms.

He could not resist a last touch of her cheek. A last quick press of his lips to hers.

God, she tasted of heaven.

"You must be tired. It was an exhausting day. I shall see you in the morning," he said, and started toward his rooms, doubting that his body would give him any rest tonight.

Just as he reached the doorway, a crash spun him about.

Eleanor stood very still, shocked by what she had done. How had it happened? One moment she had been in his arms, and then he had been pushing her away. The pain of his rejection had bit into her like a hot knife. She had been standing there, watching him walk away from her, and then red hazed her vision.

In the next instant, the figurine given them by the Cheeverlys lay in pieces on the marble hearth.

For a moment, she stared at the shards, horrified by what she had done.

Then she looked up at Lord Staines's arrested expression.

Rejection flared into hurt anger, and then into panic as she realized that she could not do what she had agreed to.

She knew how it would go. It flashed before her in an instant, like a vision, a dream that would come true. This bloodless marriage would kill her—day by day, moment by moment. Each time he turned away from her, she would die a little. Each kiss he drew back from would cut a new wound into her soul. And she would start to lash out. She would become someone she did not want to be. Someone she did not even like. She would fence off her heart, and behind those walls, cut off from light and warmth, she would die. Until only a shell existed.

"I cannot do this," she blurted out, hot tears blurring her vision. "I cannot."

"Eleanor," he said, coming to her, stretching his hands to her.

She swatted away his touch, afraid of her own longing. Afraid of his pulling away from her again. Afraid of so much.

"I lied to you. I am not sensible. I'm not anything you want, because I cannot live without love." The tears streamed down her face to fall on the carpet. She walked blindly about the room, having to move, hugging her arms, shivering with the storm of emotions that shook her.

"I thought I could do this. I thought it would be enough just to love you and not to ask or expect anything. But I cannot. You told me that I had to learn how not to care, only I do care. I care too much. And I cannot seem to stop caring, so you ought to just divorce me, or get an annulment, or whatever it is you must do to end it. For I cannot do this."

Her words ended in an anguished sob. Geoff's heart twisted. He came to her, murmuring her name. She tried to turn away from him, but he caught her in his arms.

She pushed against him. "No. It is not me you want. You don't want me at all. You never did! And I cannot bear that you do not want even to touch me, or kiss me, or . . . or anything!"

"Hush," he said, kissing the salty tear that trickled down her cheeks. "Hush, now." He kissed each tear, working from the corner of her eyes to her cheek to the corner of her mouth, to her trembling lips. And then he kissed her, full and deeply, his soul aching to stop her ache.

When he lifted his mouth, he smiled at her. "Does that feel as if I do not want you?"

She shook her head, but doubt still clouded her eyes.

Her fear echoed in him. Should he simply hold her and rock her to sleep in his arms? He wanted to do so much more, but he feared that his own selfish needs were driving him. He no longer knew what was best for either of them.

She made up his mind for him. Wrapping her arms around his neck, she pressed her lips against his and molded her soft curves to his hard planes.

"I can bear anything but to be shut out and pushed away," she murmured.

Hot longing swept through him. He caught her up in his arms, his mind still warring with his body, but his needs obliterated his hesitations. Carrying her to the bed he forgot everything but those desperate kisses.

With words he soothed her, and with his touch he stroked her skin and sought only to give them both release from these aching needs.

And as the world exploded around him, he knew he had never felt this way about any woman. The words spun in his head, but a trickle of fear returned to him even as he collapsed next to her, and even as her arms tightened around him. And he fell asleep, those words still humming in his mind and soul, but he could not trust himself to say them to her.

The distant, muffled clamor of church bells woke Eleanor. She pried open one eye, and then smiled at the weight of Geoffrey's head, pillowed against her shoulder. She liked that feeling, she realized. She had slept with her sisters when they had traveled and stopped at crowded inns. But she liked better this warm, hard feel of her husband against her side.

A flush burned across her as he shifted, brushing his hands across her naked skin. He had stripped them both bare last night, and she grew warm now with the memory of his how his hands trailed over her skin, touching her, caressing her.

Her smile widened.

If they could do this just once in a while, then she could manage to live in this marriage. The warmth brightened in her. She did not need words of love from him. No, she needed only to be able to love him. To touch him. She needed so much to give, and he had accepted everything she had offered to him as if he treasured each touch, each kiss. That would be enough for her, even if that was all he could ever give her. She felt as if she had been allowed to touch his heart, and if he could trust her so much, then she could trust him as well and had no need of armor.

The memory of how he had held her and stroked her and taken her love made her body twitch, and woke a longing that embarrassed her. Her stirring awoke her husband, and his eyes slit open, startlingly blue amid the white bed linens.

"Good morning," she whispered to him. No one would hear, but she felt as if a magic spell held them and talking too loud might shatter it. "Happy Christmas."

The glitter in his eyes deepened, and he had her tight in his arms before she could move. "Good morning, wife."

She pushed a little against him. "We ought to get up and dress before the servants arrive."

He tightened his hold. "They know better than to visit a newly married couple the morning after the wedding."

He began to nuzzle her neck, and soon had her breathless. She gave herself up to him again, her eyes closed and her body quivering.

When he lay still beside her again, she settled her cheek on his chest and wove her fingers into the hair that curled over the flat muscles there. She delighted in the male difference of him.

"I—I am sorry about last night," she said at last.

Twisting, he turned so that she lay under him and he loomed over her, propped up by his elbow and with his eyes darkening. "Never tell me you regret what we did."

"Oh, no. Not what we did. What I did. I acted awful."

A smile lifted the corner of his mouth. "Did you? Then it seems I must provoke you more often, for your awful was not so very awful that we should end up like this."

He took her hand and kissed each finger. "I said you should have a ring to match your eyes. This morning, your eyes have golden sparkles in them, just like this diamond."

She sat up, hugging the sheets with one hand and holding out her ring to watch it wink in the dawn's light. "Diamond? I thought it was a topaz. I thought that . . ."

"That I did not think you precious enough?" he finished for her. "Well, I shall buy you diamonds and emeralds and rubies and shower you in precious stones. What say you to that?"

Her cheeks warmed. "I . . . I have a present for you as well."

Slipping out of bed, she darted across the cold room.

Geoff watched with satisfaction as his wife's sweet naked figure danced to her writing desk. She came back as quickly as she had left, shivering from the morning chill, a small box in her hands.

Slipping back under the covers, she pressed her cooled skin against his and gave him the box. "Here. I had not thought to give it to you, but . . . well, I want to give you things to please you, too."

Leaning on his elbow, he flipped open the box. With thumb and forefinger, he pulled out the watch chain. On the end dangled a glass sphere.

"Your mistletoe berry?" he said, and then he looked down into her face.

She nodded, her cheeks pink. "I . . . I wanted your kisses to last forever. There, now you know how very unsensible I am. I promise I will not plague you with my . . ."

She broke off her words, looking down and biting her lower lip. He put a finger under her chin and lifted her face, pulling her gaze up to meet his.

"About what, Eleanor? Tell me now what it is that you really want. What did you write on your card and then blot out? I think I know, but I would rather hear it from you."

A flush spread from her throat to her cheeks. She looked down and began to tug at the lace trim on the pillows. "I . . . I did not have the courage to ask you for what I really wanted."

He brushed a lock of hair from her forehead. "And do you now?"

Glancing up at him she nodded. And then smiled. "I

wanted your love so desperately. Too desperately. But I vow not to pester you for I know that you do not really want . . ."

He silenced her words with a kiss. A very long kiss, and when he pulled back, he told her with a frown, "Now, tell me what I do not want."

Shyly, she smiled up at him. "Well, of course you want that. You're a man."

His arms tightened around her. "Yes, I am a man. A man who has enough sense to know when he has a wife to treasure." His eyes darkened and he smoothed a strand of hair from her forehead. "I was a man who was too stupid to see his own need, and a man too blinded by past infatuations to recognize what very precious gifts were being held out to me. But, thank God, I could open my eyes and see you before it was too late."

He folded her against his body, fitting her to him. *A perfect fit,* she thought, a deep sigh of contentment settling into her bones.

Then he pushed her back, and glared at her. "I love you, Eleanor. I do not even know when I fell in love with you. Perhaps when you rescued that damn donkey of yours. Or perhaps it was last night. I do not know. But I do know that I do not want to hear any more talk of annulments and divorce. And I do not want to hear about what I want or do not want from your lips. Allow me, please, to tell you that what I want is the sweetest love I have ever known."

She swallowed the lump in her throat.

"What's this? More tears?" he asked, frowning suddenly.

She shook her head. "No. It is only my happiness leaking out this time."

Smiling at her, he kissed each eyelid. "I did not think it at the time, but now I do. I must be the luckiest devil alive to have had the wrong woman reject me, and to have had my father twist my arm into meeting my fate—and that is you, you know."

She snuggled closer to him, pressing her body against his, delight dancing in her heart. "You are not just saying that?"

He pulled away from her. With a glance at the trapped mistletoe berry, he set it aside and then came back to her arms.

"You do not need mistletoe to have my kisses last forever, Eleanor. But in case you need reassurance of that. . . ."

With the church bells ringing for Christmas, he took her into his arms, and set about showing her that not only would his kisses last forever. His love would last much longer than that.

AUTHOR'S NOTE

As with any customs, wedding and Christmas traditions have changed over time.

In ancient days, a Christmas wedding would have been impossible for the English Church held a "closed season" on marriages from Advent in late November until St. Hilary's Day in January. The Church of England gave up such a ban during and after Cromwell's era, even though the Roman Catholic Church continued its enforcement.

Oddly enough, a custom I expected to be ancient—that of the bride having "something borrowed, something blue, and a sixpence in her shoe"—turned out to be a Victorian invention.

For Christmas customs I relied on those that have carried down through the ages: the Yule log from Viking winter solstice celebrations, the ancient Saxon decorations of holly and ivy, and the Celtic use of mistletoe on holy days, which transformed itself into a kissing bough.

I love to hear from readers, and please feel free to write and ask for instructions on playing the ancient game of Snapdragon.

Shannon Donnelly
P.O. Box 3313
Burbank, CA 91508-3313
read@shannondonnelly.com
http://www.shannondonnelly.com

More Zebra Regency Romances